About the Author

Martin Spice lived in Kathmandu for a total of nine years and travelled to Tibet twice. He is an author, journalist and reviewer whose work has regularly appeared in the Times Educational Supplement, The Weekly Telegraph, The South China Morning Post, Kitchen Garden, Grow Your Own and numerous other publications. He is also the author of *Spade, Seed & Supper: An Allotment Year*.

Also by Martin Spice

Spade, Seed & Supper: An Allotment Year

LYNX: Back to the Wild

Martin Spice

Here's hoping this brings back a few good memories!

ISBN-13 978-1530636921
ISBN -10 1530636922
Copyright © Martin Spice 2016
All rights reserved. No part of this publication may be reproduced, stored in a retrieval system or transmitted, in any form or by any means, without the prior permission of the author, nor be otherwise circulated in any form of binding or cover other than that in which it is published and without a similar condition being imposed by the purchaser.

Author's Note

The story of Tashi was told to me by friends in Kathmandu, to whom this book is dedicated. I have happy memories of those conversations and of Tashi himself lying in an armchair and listening intently.

A gallery of their original photographs of Tashi can be found at www.martinspice.com

This book would never have seen the light of day were it not for the constant urgings of my wife, Jenny. She was also untiring in her support of the writing and editing process. It is in every way her book.

Chapter One

It was cold. Sonam pulled his blanket tighter around his shoulders and shivered. His face was burning in the heat of the fire but somehow his back was still icy. High on the Tibetan plateau the winds could really howl and, even on a day as hot as this one had been, the early evening breeze was enough to chill. Behind him, just outside the tent where his family lived in the summer months, his mother was preparing the evening meal. He was already hungry and the drifting smell of the smoke and grilled meat was almost unbearable.

    The meat was a rare treat. Usually they would eat tsampa, ground barley mixed with water. But today was different. It was late October and the time had come to slaughter the sheep they had so carefully herded over the last few months. Sonam looked around their campsite. There was still blood on the ground in places. He hated much of what he had witnessed that day. For many months he had helped drive their sheep from pasture to pasture, letting them crop the thin grass that grew only when the ground was not covered in ice and snow. He knew all the sheep individually and had given them names, although he had not told his father that. He would not have approved. And then that morning his father had got out his long knife and started to kill and skin the sheep.

At first Sonam had not been able to watch. The bleating cries of the sheep had filled the air and he had turned away, sickened by the sight of blood and the animals' obvious distress. But his father had called him over to help and spoken to him sharply.

"What's the matter with you? You scared of the sight of a little blood? You'll be happy enough to eat the meat, won't you?"

He had not answered.

"What's the matter with you, I said?" His father was getting angry. "Come and help. There's a lot of work to do today and it has to be done quickly. Do you want the animals to suffer more than they have to?"

And so Sonam had swallowed his fear and gone to help. His father had been less angry with him then. His mother had crouched beside him as they worked paring skin from flesh and looked at him kindly. She knew her son. Although Sonam had watched this every year, he had never liked it. She had explained it all to him before and he understood. He knew that they could not herd the sheep in winter when the winds screamed across the frozen Tibetan plateau and the snow drifted tens of feet deep. There would be nothing for the sheep to eat and they would die wretched deaths. The family would keep the breeding ewes in the rough stone shelter that adjoined their draughty winter home but the rest of the flock would be butchered or sold.

"We cannot let the sheep starve and we cannot starve either," she had explained. "We need the meat for the long winter months. It needs to be dried now, whilst there is still sun hot enough to do it. We will keep what we need and sell the rest. We have to live, Sonam, and we are very poor."

He knew in his head she was right, although his heart still ached at the sight and smell of so much death. And so, when that morning his father had sharpened his knife, his eyes had filled with tears that he had quickly blinked away. His mother had been right. They had to live.

But now it was evening and the day's work was over. He sat by the fire in front of the tent and looked into the distance. For a long way the land was grey and flat before it finally rose to meet the mountains in the distance. To one side of him was the wooden structure he had helped his father to build. It was a tripod of three poles tied together with rope at each end and a single bar across the top. From the bar hung the carcasses of three sheep. They would hang there for the wind and sun to dry them so they could be stored for winter.

"Sonam!" His mother was calling. There were delicious smells coming from the inside of the tent where she was cooking. "Go and get me some water. The food's nearly ready."

He sighed. There was no rest. Whenever he started to daydream he was interrupted. He picked up the plastic water container and set off to the nearby stream.

"Nima!" He called up his dog. She had been his best friend for as long as he could remember and he could not recall a time when she had not been there. They went everywhere together. She was brown and black, big and powerful, with a rough coat and shiny eyes. A mastiff, bred to guard the sheep and their owners, a fighter ready to attack any hungry leopard or wild cat that had its eyes on the sheep. To strangers she was fierce. Sonam had often wondered why she barked and snarled so ferociously when anyone came near their tent but as he got older he had understood that she was simply protecting him and his family. Now he was grateful to her.

As it was getting dusk, he fastened her night-time collar around her neck. It was a band of thick leather through which dozens of two inch nails had been driven, their sharp points facing outwards from her bristling neck. Every time Sonam put this on her he told her the same story.

"Now, Nima, it is time to wear your collar. Soon it will be night and the wild animals will start to stalk around us. Your job is to protect the sheep. A leopard could kill you if you don't wear your collar but with these spikes nothing can get a grip on your throat. So you must wear this to stop anything attacking you." And this evening, like every other, Nima stood patiently while Sonam attached the collar and soothed her with words she could not understand. Then she bounded ahead of him, turning to look over her shoulder to make sure she was going the right way.

Right now he was headed for the stream down a steep and slippery track. He threw a stone for Nima and she chased after it, watching it fall and roll in the dirt. He slid down the last few feet to the stream, bent down and carefully filled the container from the little waterfall that served as his tap. He was just about to turn back and go home when he noticed Nima sniffing interestedly at the mud, her nose almost buried in the ground. He called to her but she paid no attention. With thoughts of cooked meat filling his head and a rumble in his tummy, he was in no mood, for once, to loiter. "Come on," he shouted. But she didn't move. "Come on!" He was getting irritated now and went over to drag her away from whatever it was she found so interesting.

It was a paw print, etched quite clearly in the mud. He bent down and examined it carefully. A large cat. A very large cat. Not quite big enough for an adult leopard but maybe a young one? Suddenly he felt scared. Looking around he could see nothing but the stream, a couple of low shrubs, some big rocks, dust. But Sonam was not fooled. He knew a leopard could lie low and be almost invisible. It could easily be watching him, eyeing him up, contemplating an attack. Yelling at Nima to follow him, he picked up the water container and took it as fast as he could back to camp.

He gave the water to his mother and then sat down again by the fire. Now that he was back safely, he wondered what animal had made the tracks. And, more of a problem, whether he should tell his father. He knew, of course, that he should. Although some of the sheep had been slaughtered, many more were still alive. If a big cat was hanging around the tents, it was for one reason only. He knew that they could not afford the loss of even one sheep and often an attack would kill more than one. Yet if he told his father, his father would try and trap it. To kill a big cat was to make money. The skin was valuable and could be sold and the bones were worth many dollars. They would be sold to a man who would sell them on to a Chinese trader. Then they would be made into medicines, perhaps to sell in Hong Kong or one of the big cities Sonam had heard about but never seen. He was torn. He should tell his father so the sheep could be protected; on the other hand, he did not want the animal to be killed. What should he do?

His thoughts were interrupted by his mother.

"Sonam, food!" And there in front of him was a dish piled high with the fresh mutton momos that his mother had been making. Minced meat, mixed with wild herbs, wrapped in a thin white dough and then steamed, they were the most delicious food he had ever tasted. When they ate like this, they ate like kings, his father had told him, and they only ate like kings a few times in the year. Sonam stared at the pile on his plate and then started eating. He ate until nothing was left. So absorbed was he in his eating that he did not really notice his family around him or the voices of the families in the neighbouring tents.

When he had finished, he slowly returned to the outside world. His father was talking to his friend Renzing. "There's something around. Last night I couldn't sleep and I could hear something outside and Nima was restless. I could hear her whining in that low whimpering voice she has when she picks up a scent she doesn't like. If it hadn't been so cold I would have gone to look. Not that there would have been much point, I suppose."

Renzing was looking worried. And Sonam realised that if he was going to tell them what he had seen, he had to do it now. Both men looked at him when he spoke.

"When I went to get the water..." he began reluctantly.

"Yes?"

"When I went to get the water," Sonam repeated, "Nima found a print. A paw print. It was pretty big," he added.

"Where? Where exactly?" His father's voice had quickened with interest.

"Down by the stream. Where I get the water." Sonam knew what would follow now. He suddenly felt tired and a little sick. He was not used to rich food like this and the knowledge of what he had said was beginning to hurt him.

"Show me." His father was already on his feet.

"It's too dark." But even as he said it, he knew it was no good. His father would not be talked out of it now. And in truth it was only dusk, not yet fully dark. They would be able to see alright. Reluctantly he got up and left the heat of the fire behind him. His father was in the tent, looking through one of the big wood and leather trunks in which they stored their possessions. With a heavy heart, Sonam knew he was looking for his old gun and his snares.

They called Nima and set off for the stream, Sonam leading the way, slipping on the dry dust of the path and skidding almost out of control until his father caught his arm and steadied him. He was a stern man but a kindly one. There was something about his son he had never really understood. Everyone liked Sonam but somehow he was never fully involved in camp life with the other kids' games and practical jokes. He seemed happy just to sit by the fire and dream. Strange.

While he had been thinking this, Nima had run on ahead. Suddenly she froze, crouching down almost flat to the ground, her ears lying back against her head. Her lips were drawn back into a snarl but no sound came from her throat. Sonam and his father stood still. Slowly Nima moved forward. Something was ahead. But it was too dark to see clearly in the fading light and after a moment Nima relaxed. Whatever had been there, had gone.

By the side of the stream, Sonam showed his father the paw print. He had thought he might lie, say he couldn't find the place, that he must have been mistaken. But Nima's reaction to what she had sensed had convinced his father that the sheep might be in real danger. He bent down and stared, squinting his eyes in the twilight; then he touched the print and smelled his fingers. He looked around the area carefully, finding another print and some scat. Finally he turned to Sonam.

"You've done well. I'm not sure what this is. I don't think it's big enough for a snow leopard but it's certainly a big cat and it's obviously attracted by our sheep. I'll set some snares. If nothing else, its skin will make a good hat for the winter." He grinned at Sonam and then bent down to place the thin wires that he hoped would trap the animal as it ranged through the dark.

He worked carefully in the near darkness for about half an hour. He was a skilled trapper and he knew the habits of wild animals. He positioned the loops of wire in the undergrowth at the places where the animal might come down to the water to drink. Then he covered them with leaves and dust to hide them as best he could. Finally he stood up.

"Come on Sonam, let's go. And maybe by tomorrow one of us will have the fur for a fine new hat."

Chapter Two

That night Sonam could hardly sleep. He tossed and turned under the thin blanket and the heavy animal skins. Once he woke up suddenly, convinced that he had heard the cry of an animal in pain. But though he listened intently he could hear nothing.

He turned over to sleep again but he slept badly, his slumber haunted by dreams. He was alone in a dark wood. He had been walking for hours and he was nearly exhausted. He had only gone down to the stream to get water – how could he have got so lost? Still, there was nothing he could do but carry on. But why was it taking so long to get anywhere? Suddenly he thought he glimpsed a dark shape move behind a tree. He shivered. He was not cold but he was sure something was watching him. He spun around but there was nothing. His fear increased and he started running. Frantically, he ran towards the only break in the trees he could see, tripping and stumbling as he ran. He could hear breathing behind him now but he was too scared to turn around. Surely whatever it was must catch him. And then he was on the ground too terrified to move. There was silence. Very slowly he opened his eyes. The wood had vanished and in its place was a field or perhaps a garden. There were flowers and grass. In front of him was a white house with a golden roof and flowers growing in boxes at its windows. Sonam had never seen anything so beautiful. He stood up and made his way towards it...

"Sonam! Sonam!" His father's voice woke him. "Come on, get up. Come on you good for nothing; let's see if the gods have put anything in our snares."

Sonam got up reluctantly. His mother gave him hot salty tea and he drank it slowly, trying to hold in his mind the image of the beautiful house. But like all images from dreams it faded quickly and he was back in the cramped tent, seated by a pile of skins, his breath making patterns in the chill morning air.

His father was waiting impatiently, stamping his feet outside.

Finally, Sonam was ready and he and his father set out together, Sonam carrying the water container whilst Nima ran around them in circles, glad to be free from the long daytime chain that kept her close to the tent. He knew in his heart what they would find and as they splashed across the stream he thought he could see something moving in the undergrowth. But he wasn't sure.

His father was busy checking the snares. He had set three and already he had brushed away the leaves and grass that hid the treacherous wires of the first two. There had been nothing. "Perhaps I'll be lucky," Sonam thought, "and the third will be empty as well."

But his hopes were shattered by his father's excited cry. "Come here Sonam, look at this! What a catch!"

As slowly as he dared, Sonam went to join his father. He could see him bent over something in the grass but whatever it was, it wasn't moving. He went closer. And then he was staring at the animal that lay there. It was big but not as big as a snow leopard. It was a cat alright, one with pointed ears and a short stubby tail. It had obviously been dead for some time for when Sonam bent forward to touch it, it was cold. The wire of the snare was around its neck. The peg that held the snare was still in the ground but it was loose. If the animal had just pulled harder it would have broken free with the wire tight around its neck. Sonam was pleased that had not happened. If the animal had to die, better that it die quickly. But he turned his eyes away from the lips curled back in pain and the glazed eyes that, even in death, held terror.

His father was excited. In a hard winter, the money he could get for the skin and bones could make all the difference between bare survival and comfort. His eyes shone as he congratulated Sonam on spotting the paw marks. He was not a cruel man and he neither liked nor disliked the killing. It was simply his way of life, as it had been his father's before him. He had already taken his knife from his belt and was preparing to skin the cat.

"What is it?" Sonam asked.

"It's a lynx. And look at how her teats are swollen. She must have had a cub not long ago." But he was not really interested in any cub at that moment. As he sharpened his knife on a stone his head was full of the extra dollars the skin would bring. "A snow leopard would have been better but this is still good. I can get maybe $20 for the skin and $10 a kilo for the bones. But we have to go to Shigatse to sell them there. Now don't disturb me while I work. One slip of the knife and the skin will be worth nothing."

Sonam watched and, although the sight of the dead animal saddened him, he had to admire his father's skill and the way in which the skin slipped off the animal as if it were a coat.

"There," said his father as he held up the pelt, "a perfect job."

The skin was about a metre long and over half a metre wide. The colour was greyish yellow and there was no obvious pattern to the spots. It felt very soft to touch. But what Sonam noticed most were the ears with their black tufted points.

His father was stretching the skin out flat on the ground, examining its size. He looked happy.

"This will make someone a fine hat. But we can't use it, Sonam. We'll take the money because it's of more use to us. Some rich man may wear it on his head or some rich woman could wear it around her neck. For them it's fashion, for us it's food and warmth."

Sonam was surprised to hear his father say so much. Usually he was silent, except when he drank with his friends and then he often argued fiercely and loudly. But the rest of the time he was a man of few words.

As if he thought he had said too much, his father turned his attention to the carcass. With his knife he began carefully to remove all the flesh and the innards until nothing was left but the bones. They gleamed white and looked surprisingly thin and fragile. Then his father took the skin and carefully wrapped the bones inside it. He washed his knife thoroughly in the stream and called Sonam. He was ready to go back to their tent.

"Come on Sonam, let's go. This meat will fry up nicely for breakfast. It'll give you the strength and agility of a cat and prevent a hundred diseases."

Father and son climbed the path steadily. It was getting warmer now as the sun rose and Sonam could see the snow on the high mountains in the distance sparkling in the early morning light. At the top of the path he stopped and looked back at the stream. The guts of the lynx lay in a neat pile on the ground where his father had left them, waiting to be eaten by one or more of the vultures that were always circling in the clear blue mountain air. Sonam looked at them and then into the bushes that bordered the stream. For a moment he thought he saw something move but when he squinted harder there was nothing. He must have been mistaken. His father was well ahead of him by now and he ran to catch up.

Breakfast that morning was a cheerful affair although Sonam had difficulty in swallowing the meat. But his father insisted it was good for him and it didn't actually taste too bad once you forgot what it was. His father had proudly unrolled the skin to show his mother and they weighed the bones carefully in their hands to try and guess how much they might be worth. They talked excitedly of the things they could buy when they reached the town – perhaps some new plastic buckets, a warm coat and a Buddhist amulet for good luck.

They were to spend just one more night where they were and then they would set off for Shigatse. There were more sheep to be slaughtered but when the carcasses had dried overnight and in the next day's sun, the ponies would be loaded with their tent and the rest of their belongings. Even the remaining sheep would carry packs on their backs. It was Sonam's job to drive them along whilst his father led the ponies. It would take them several days to reach the city but time was not important. For Sonam, the city was only a distant memory. Last year they had not gone, he and his mother, although his father had done some trading there. He was not sure what he thought about it all. Shigatse was noisy with people and cars and he was happiest in quiet places. Still, he had other things to worry about for the next few days.

Throughout the day he helped his father. They dealt with the sheep quickly and efficiently and by mid-morning there were two more carcasses hanging from the tripod and drying in the open air. His mother was busy scrubbing the pans and tin plates, cooking the food and packing away into trunks the things they would not need that night. The next morning would be hard work as they rolled up the tent and loaded the animals. They would start long before it was fully light.

As the afternoon slipped away, Sonam lay on his back in the sun and stared up into the blue of the sky. He drifted away nicely until his mother called him. "Sonam! Stop daydreaming and fetch me some more water from the stream. And while you are at it, have a good wash."

He sighed as he picked up the water container and set off on the now familiar path.

He slithered down the bank. He was fond of this stream and of the rocks and pools where the water flowed. The guts of the lynx had already disappeared and a small dark stain was the only trace of where they had been. He filled the water container and then remembered that he had to wash as well. The sun was sinking rapidly and if he was not quick it would soon be too cold. The little valley trapped the sun but the moment it was in shadow the temperature would drop. He looked at the stream. He knew just how cold this mountain water was. But his mother would scold him if he did not at least look as though he had scrubbed himself clean. He splashed water over his face and neck and rubbed his hands together under the small waterfall. The water ran brown before it swirled away downstream. He thought of taking off his shirt but hesitated. She would never check. He opened the top two buttons and splashed water on his chest, inhaling sharply from the cold. That would pass unless she decided to give him a thorough inspection and with a busy moving day coming up, that seemed unlikely.

He did up the buttons again and sat down on the bank. His feet were trailing in the water and were going slightly numb. The sun was warm on his back and he felt sleepy. It had been a busy day. Only half awake now, he lay on the bank and listened to the sound of the running water...

When he awoke some time later, the sun was low in the sky. It was getting dark quickly. He sat up and started to put his shoes back on but first he had to rub his feet to get the blood moving. His shoes were torn and worn through but they did offer a little protection against the cold and the rough ground. He was lucky to have some, he knew – some of the other boys had to go barefoot.

He bent down to pick up the water container. As he did so he thought he saw something move in the bushes. This was ridiculous. Why did he always think he saw things? He was about to turn away when the movement caught his eye again.

"You idiot," he said aloud to himself. But he went to look anyway.

Bending down he brushed the grass and thin branches to one side. And then Sonam drew in his breath and for a whole minute just stood and stared.

For in the grass at his feet, hissing through its tiny pointed teeth, was the baby cub of the snared lynx.

Chapter Three

For several days the cub lived inside Sonam's jacket as they walked towards the city of Shigatse. Although at first it had hissed and clawed at him when he tried to pick it up, the cub was really too small to do any damage and Sonam soon learned to ignore its protests despite the occasional scratches from the sharp little claws. And over the days, the cub's protests disappeared altogether as it came to realise that Sonam was the source of its warmth and food.

The journey was a long one. After four days they came to some flat land near a river. As it was already late in the afternoon they decided to stop there for the night. Over supper his father told Sonam that they would reach Shigatse the following day.

That night, Sonam sat by the fire for even longer than usual. It was not as cold here as it had been on the plateau and the grey rock and the dust of the hills had changed to greenery. There were trees by the side of the rough track road and instead of big empty spaces there were neat fields where barley grew. Instead of stained and cramped tents, the people had low houses with firewood stacked on the roofs ready for the cold of the coming winter.

They had pitched their tent in the field of a friendly villager, who had also lent them a hut in which to herd their remaining sheep. There was water nearby and in the evening the whole village met to talk and swap stories. Life in the valleys seemed so much easier than living in the mountains.

It was not long before he started to feel dozy in front of the fire. Travelling was hard even when you were used to it. Getting up before first light, packing, herding the animals, loading them up and then walking all day before doing all the same things in reverse. No wonder he was tired.

Half asleep, he stared into the embers of the fire. And slowly they changed before his eyes. Bits of charred wood and glowing flame formed into golden shapes that twisted and grew. Sonam gasped. There it was again, as clear and sharp as it had been before in his dream: the white house with its golden roof in a garden of flowers and trees. It was so real that he almost got up to walk towards it. And as he watched, a strange feeling of peace crept over him. He had not felt like this before. It was as if he and the fire and the night were one.

Lost in his dream world, Sonam felt his mother shaking him gently. "Poor boy. You're falling asleep. Go into the tent and lie down." Reluctantly he stirred himself to do as he was told. He cuddled the cub to him as he went inside and its head was still nuzzled into the warmth of his body when he went to sleep.

It seemed no time before his mother was waking him.

"Sonam! Sonam! Come on! Up! It's time to get up!" She held out a tin mug of buttery tea to him. "Come on! What's wrong with you? Are you ill?"

No, thought Sonam, I am not ill but I am sick. His sleep had been broken up with worry. Today they would arrive in the city. Some of the dried meat would be sold and some of the live sheep too if the price was right. The skin of the lynx would be sold and so would its bones. These things he knew and understood. It hurt to watch the sheep being sold but he knew it must happen. No, these things were inevitable. But what about the cub?

His father had said he could keep it until they reached the city – and then he would see.

What did that mean? That he would see if there was a good price to be had for it? That if he got a good price for the sheep and the bones he would not need the money for the cub? Or that he would see if he could find a buyer and sell it? So could he keep the cub or would he have to let it go? These thoughts had tormented him all night. He ached over the not-knowing. And if he did have to let it go, what would happen to it? Would someone buy it and keep it as a pet? Or... But Sonam could hardly let the other possibilities stay in his mind.

He took the cub from under the pile of skins and blankets where it had burrowed and placed it gently on the ground. It could crawl but it could not walk properly. At first he had thought it would die. After the first bout of hissing, it had simply gone limp and looked as if it were half dead already. His father and mother had doubted that it would live. But Sonam had cared for it well. He had forced open its mouth until it had taken some drops of sheep's milk. Then he had fed it every few hours until slowly the cub had gained in strength. It had opened its eyes and stared at Sonam and then it had slept. He smiled to himself as he remembered those first days. But what would happen now?

When a few hours later they entered the city, Sonam's heart was no lighter. His father was in high spirits as they had already sold their spare meat and three of their surplus sheep. Business had been good. The prices were higher than they had been the year before, much higher, and the thought of the oncoming winter was suddenly less threatening. His mother had spent time talking to some of her friends in the town and shopping in the marketplace while his father had finished his business in the shed that sold great pots of tomba, an alcoholic drink made from millet. When he had finally left his new found friends, he was flushed with the success of his trading.

"Come on, Sonam. It's time to see an old man about these bones," and he strode off up the street before Sonam had even had time to work out what he meant.

They left the main street and turned into an alleyway so narrow that Sonam's shoulders almost touched the walls on both sides. For his father, a few yards ahead of him, it was a real squeeze. Then he disappeared. One minute he was there, the next he was gone. Sonam rushed to where he had last seen him and found a narrow flight of steep steps. He could not see his father at the bottom of them but there was nowhere else he could have gone. Sonam started down.

At the bottom, at right angles to the steps, was a doorway a little smaller than Sonam himself. He squeezed through and stood up in a room that stank with a smell that turned his stomach, a sharp smell of death and decay. All around him were bottles and jars. As he looked more closely he realised they were full of creatures that had once been alive. He had no names for many of them but he recognised a snake and some insects, what looked like an unborn lamb and some other parts he could not identify but had obviously come from some poor animal. He looked in fascination and horror. All these lives in all these jars; all these creatures swimming in a sickly pale liquid that disguised any colour and turned everything in them to a watery yellow.

His eyes moved to the table. On it were the skins of animals he had never seen, although he recognised them from the stories his father had told him. The pale spotted one must be a snow leopard and the darker ones wildcats. There was something that looked like a small bear, white at the edges with a wide dark brown and black stripe that ran the length of it. He had seen such a creature once but he did not know its name. To the left of the table were more jars and tins. He turned slowly to where his father was sitting.

Opposite his father was a small man dressed in a long black robe. It was open at the front and underneath it he wore a collection of shirts and pullovers. All of them were stained. They were not worn and threadbare like his father's clothes but simply shabby. He was looking at his father through his thin wire framed glasses. His eyes were red and watery. A small beard sprouted in wispy hairs from his unshaven chin. He had barely glanced at Sonam when he came in and he ignored him now, staring instead at his father with a cold appraising scrutiny.

"Skin and bones," he was saying. "Well, there are skins and there are bones. Let me see what you have." He tapped his fingers impatiently on the table as if Sonam's father were taking up his valuable time.

His father took the bundle from inside his jacket and laid the skin out carefully on the table, placing the bones in front of the shopkeeper, who prodded them and turned them over contemptuously with his finger. "These," he said, "these are worth very little. There is no market for them. Now if they had been tiger bones I could have paid you a good price. But a lynx? Who would want the bones of a lynx?"

He pushed them to one side. "Now let me see this skin you have made so much of." He smoothed it down on the table, stretching it out, fur side up. Then he turned it over to look at the flesh side. He felt it under his fingers. Slowly he shook his head.

"The skin is of no more use than the bones. See, feel here. It's hard. To make a coat or a hat it must be soft and pliable. You have not cured this properly. You left it out in the hot sun. Now it is hard. Who will buy such a thing?"

Sonam looked at his father. His face was drawn and his eyes had lost the sparkle of a few minutes before. He needed the money from this. He knew the shopkeeper would try to beat him down to a low price. He had expected that. But now it seemed that what he had was worth nothing.

"How much?" he asked. No other words would come.

"How much? How much, the man asks. To be truthful my friend I do not really want this at all. What can I do with it? Perhaps the skin will sit in my shop for months and some moth will attack it. Then no-one will ever buy it. And so I'll lose my money."

"But the bones?" his father asked.

"Ah, the bones. If only they belonged to a tiger! Look. You are a poor man and you need the money. I can give you something. Not because what you try to sell me is worth anything but for charity, from the goodness of my heart."

"How much will you give?"

"How much charity does a rich man give a beggar?"

But the shopkeeper had gone too far. His father was angry now at the insult and started to roll up the bones in the skin. The shopkeeper put up his hand to stop him. He was smiling now, his yellow discoloured teeth gleaming dully in the half-darkness.

"Stop, my friend, do not be hasty." He looked at Sonam. "Do not let your fine boy starve because of your pride. Perhaps I can find a buyer for the skin, poor though it is. Perhaps when they are ground up no-one will know the difference between tiger bone and lynx. Perhaps." And then he looked hard and straight at the poor man in front of him. "And perhaps," he said softly, "the winter will be harder than you think."

For a moment Sonam thought his father was going to take the skin and bones away. But there was defeat in his face.

"How much?" he asked again.

"I can give you ten dollars."

"Is that all?" His father knew he was being cheated but he also knew he could do nothing about it. He could try to sell somewhere else but it would make no difference. All the skins and bones sold in the area eventually found their way back to this shop. The man was the heart of the trade – if such a trade could be said to have a heart.

"Make it twelve."

The shopkeeper sighed. Then he took out the money and handed it over. His father folded it carefully, tucked it into his pocket and left the shop without another word, pushing Sonam ahead of him up the steps. Halfway up, he heard his father stop.

"Sonam, wait there!"

His father went back down the steps and pushed the door open. His voice was quite clear. "How much for a live cub?"

But Sonam did not wait to hear the reply. With a cry of rage he pounded up the rest of the steps and into the alleyway. He could hear his father's footsteps behind him now and he knew he would be gaining on him. Soon he was in the wide open square. He looked back. His father was only a few metres behind him, shouting angrily, red in the face. He had been humiliated once that day by a shopkeeper and now his own son...

Sonam was desperate. He looked around frantically. He could not escape from here. Over in the far corner of the square was a big car, almost a truck. He ran towards it. The cub must not die, he kept thinking, must not die, must not end up in one of those yellow glass jars. Perhaps someone would take it. Four people were just getting out of the car. They were all *gau-serpo*, gold heads, Westerners. Exhausted and out of breath he collapsed at the feet of a middle-aged man. The man was about to push him aside – he had seen too many beggars already on this trip. And then he stopped. For in the boy's outstretched hand was the lynx cub.

Chapter Four

Much later on, Sonam would think of that day as the one that changed his life forever. But at the time such a lot happened so quickly that it was many days before he managed to sort the events out clearly. He remembered the day in pictures: the look of surprise on the tourist's face; the anger on his father's; the tears of his mother later on; the calm of the monk and the stillness of the monastery; the night filled with stars. But before he reached the peace of the beautiful sky, there had been terrible anger.

His father had arrived at the scene just as Sonam had fallen to his knees. But he was too late to stop the interest the tourists were showing in the cub.

"Oh look, isn't it sweet?" said the tall lady with the funny earrings. "What is it?" And they had talked for several minutes among themselves, passing the lynx from one to the other until the cub had grown afraid and Sonam had taken him back. At that point his father had grasped him firmly by the arm and was going to lead him away. But by then the tourists had called their guide and clearly wanted to talk to Sonam and his father.

"What are you going to do with it?"
"How did you find it?"

"Where's its mother?"

With a slightly impatient look, the guide translated their questions.

"I found it down by the stream on the mountain, after we snared its mother," explained Sonam.

This was not the answer the tourists wanted to hear and they muttered angrily about endangered species.

"What will you do with it now?"

Sonam had looked fearfully at his father.

"It will be sold..." but before his father could finish the sentence Sonam could restrain himself no longer.

"It will be sold to an evil old man who lives down there," he burst out, pointing down the street to the alleyway. "He lives in a stinking room full of dead animals. Smelly skins. He has things pickled in jars. He's a horrible ugly old man. I hate him. He'll kill the cub and put it in a jar." And as he said the words, Sonam suddenly covered his eyes with his arm and started to cry.

The tourists were concerned. One put his arm around Sonam's shoulders while another continued to talk to his father through the guide.

"Why do you want to sell the cub? How much will you get for it?"

And Sonam's father explained as best he could that the winter was coming and that they were very poor. He told the tourists, through their guide, about how they lived for much of the year in a tent and had almost no money. And how, to them, the trapping of a lynx or a leopard was like a gift from the gods because it meant that the winter would be less hard and they would have warm clothes and more food. And besides, a lynx would attack their sheep...

Sonam was watching the tourists and could see that they did not like what they were hearing. Clearly they did not approve of the death of the mother lynx. But he could also see them beginning to nod their heads as they listened to his father's descriptions of their family life. They could understand that the trapping was more necessity than greed.

When his father had finished and the guide had translated the bits he thought were the most important, the man Sonam had first run into turned to him. He was a big man and Sonam found him quite frightening. "My name is Chuck. You are Sonam?"

Sonam nodded as he heard his name and smiled back weakly. Chuck turned to the guide. "How much will he get for the cub?" The guide passed on the question.

"Ten dollars," said Sonam's father.

"Fifteen dollars," said the guide, adding a bit on for himself. If there was going to be a sale he would be happy to make something out of it.

Again the tourists talked amongst themselves. They were looking serious and seemed to Sonam to be arguing. He shifted from foot to foot, impatient to get away but fearful of what his father was going to do to him once the tourists had gone. Every now and then one of them would turn to the guide and ask another question: "Is there any law about taking an animal from Tibet to Nepal?"

"How thorough are Customs on the Nepalese side of the border?"

They asked so many questions these *gau-serpo*. What time would they get to Kathmandu? How long were they staying there on this trip? What time was their flight out?

Sonam tried at first to follow the conversation, turning his head to look at each person as they spoke but understanding nothing of what was said. So many questions that he did not understand. In fact, as the discussion continued and the arguments went back and forth, he simply felt sad and forgotten. His father and the guide were busy talking and, from the bit he could hear of what they said, he gathered that the tourists were thinking of taking the cub with them to Nepal. They were driving overland to Kathmandu and would be there in just over two days. One of them had a friend there who might just possibly...

At last the group seemed to reach some kind of agreement. The guide explained. "They will give you ten dollars for the cub. They want to try and save it from certain death. One of them has a friend in Kathmandu and he thinks that he may agree to look after it. He is Buddhist so he probably thinks it will be good for his karma and earn him merit in his next life." The guide laughed at this; he had no such beliefs himself.

Sonam's father was too experienced a trader to give in so easily. Almost without thinking he said, "Tell them the price is fifteen dollars. What is ten dollars to them? Their gloves cost more than that."

The guide told the group that the price had changed. They scowled at Sonam and his father but in the end four five dollar bills changed hands, the guide discreetly diverting one of them into his own pocket. He thought he had earned it.

Sonam was pleased that he had saved the cub from the shopkeeper but he could not bring himself to smile as he handed it over. He watched as the man called Chuck emptied out a bag and lined it with a towel before carefully laying the cub inside. There was care in his hands and concern in his face but the cub had been with Sonam for many days and it was his in a way it would never be anyone else's. He watched as the group climbed back into their Landcruiser and drove off through the square. He tried not to let his father see the tears in his eyes.

Once they were out of sight, Sonam felt the full force of his father's anger. Although he'd made more money as a result of what had happened, it did not alter the fact that Sonam had disobeyed him and run away.

"You made me look stupid in front of that shopkeeper," his father spat. "In front of that evil-minded thief. He wanted the cub. I turned around to get it from you and you were gone, running away from me like a street boy who has picked a pocket. You will not do that. You will never do that. You will do as I say, when I say it. You are my son and you will obey me whether you think I am right or not. Whether you agree or not. Do you understand me Sonam? Or shall I make you understand another way?"

His arm was raised to hit Sonam. But as if from nowhere his mother was suddenly at his side. She turned on his father, much to the amusement of the growing crowd of people who had stopped to watch this family quarrel.

"What's the matter with you? Sonam loved the cub, can't you see that? He wanted to save it but you were going to have it killed. No wonder the boy is upset. What is the matter with you? We've got more money and the cub has a chance of living. You should be celebrating, not quarrelling like dogs in the street for everyone to watch."

His father stared at her for a moment. "You always stick up for the boy," he said, then he turned and walked away. He would go and get drunk now and then he would be alright. Though his temper was fierce, it soon passed.

"Come Sonam," his mother said, "the buying and the selling is finished. This is a place of pilgrimage. Once, before the Chinese came, the monastery of Shigatse had over four thousand monks. Now it is still a holy place but..."

She talked as she guided him gently through the market. The goods for sale were spread out along the sides of the street. There were stalls selling vegetables and fruit, household goods, yak butter, salt and meat. There were Chinese pullovers and coats. He passed a shop selling pots of noodles but in spite of his hesitation and longing looks his mother did not stop. She wanted to leave all this behind and go through the great doors of the monastery.

Tashilhunpo Monastery is a town of its own. It has its own streets and its own steps and staircases and dark lanes and alleys. It is a very easy place to get lost if you do not know your way around – and that is exactly what Sonam did.

At first he had followed his mother as she went up the steps and into the Hall of Maitreya. It was huge, richly painted in oranges, blues and gold. Inside was the most gigantic Buddha he had ever seen. This was Champa, the Buddha of the Future, his mother had explained. But Sonam was overawed by its size. The monks who sat in front of it, chanting, came barely to the height of the Buddha's toe. His eyes travelled slowly upwards, over the knees and the arms and the chest. By the time they got to the peaceful face at the top, his head was bent so far back that his neck hurt. He walked around the back of the statue. The chanting of the monks was making him feel strange and the smell of the burning butter lamps filled his brain.

Behind the statue, where it was darkest, he almost tripped and put out a hand to steady himself. His hand reached for the wall but there was nothing there and he fell onto some steps that were set into the wall. Without thinking, he started to climb.

The steps were steep and spiralled round until they came to a small platform. Sonam stood on it and looked down. Now it was obvious to him – the steps climbed up alongside the Buddha. So far he was only ten metres or so above the ground. He looked up. The Buddha's head was still a long way above him. He looked down again to check that his mother was still praying. She was. It would be some time before she missed him. He carried on up the staircase. It got narrower and the spirals got tighter. This section seemed to be a lot longer. He must have climbed over two hundred steps by now and surely must be near the top? He was just at the point of giving up and going back down when the staircase widened to form another platform. In front of him was a door. Sonam pushed it open, expecting to find himself staring at the head of the Buddha. Instead he was in a small room. And in the room was a monk.

When Sonam could finally see into the darkness he realised that the monk was staring at him. He was sitting cross-legged in front of a low table. To one side of him was another small image of the Buddha, in front of which were silver bowls of pure water, flowers and butter lamps.

The monk did not seem in the slightest bit surprised to see Sonam. He looked up and studied him for a moment. Then he smiled. Without saying anything, he invited him to sit down opposite him. Then after some time he spoke.

"If you have found me, you have been sent to me. Why are you troubled?"

And Sonam, who was normally shy and rarely spoke to strangers, found words pouring out of him. He could not stop talking. He told the monk about his life as a herder, about his mother and his father, about how he hated killing the sheep, about the death of the lynx, the rescue of the cub, the ugly shop-keeper and the tourists. He talked without stopping for several minutes. And finally he heard himself say, "And then there is this dream I keep having..."

"Your dream?"

And so Sonam told him of the white house with the golden roof, set in a beautiful garden with grass and flowers. When he had finished, the monk was silent for a long time. Finally he spoke.

"The place you describe is a long way from here and to reach it you will have to go on a long journey. You will make this journey. It is your fate and no-one escapes that. You are young but I sense this journey will come soon. There will be danger and you will travel much of the way alone. I cannot tell you how but the cub you have saved is in some way part of this. There is something special about you, Sonam, but you will have to find out for yourself what it is. And when you have found it, you must be true to it."

He placed his hands briefly on Sonam's head and then returned to his prayers. He did not look up as Sonam quietly left the room and went down the spiral staircase to rejoin his mother. He found her waiting below as if nothing had happened.

Chapter Five

In Kathmandu, two days later, Will Nugent was playing football in his back garden.

"G-o-a-l!!" he cried, arms stretched up into the air before sinking to his knees and sliding to a halt in front of sixty thousand adoring fans. "What a great start for Manchester United!"

He and his friend Tim had been playing football all afternoon and evening. Tim was in goal and Will was trying to settle an old score with Manchester City in the most fiercely fought of all local derbies. He had dribbled the ball skilfully through three defending flower pots and had managed to take the ball away from the rose bush with an excellent sliding tackle. Picking himself up quickly, he had struck a low shot into the bottom corner of the net, just grazing the post, leaving Tim floundering as Manchester United cemented their challenge to win the Premiership.

Well, that was what he had meant to happen.

What had actually happened was that he had tried a sliding tackle round the rose bush and torn his shorts. Ignoring that, he had struck a low hard shot that had entirely missed the goal and instead had crashed into a flowerpot full of orchids that his father had carefully brought back from some jungle trip or other. The ball had continued into the patch of vegetable garden and flattened his mother's carefully nurtured parsley. As if this wasn't bad enough, his mother had arrived at the very moment he had trampled down another of her herbs and booted the ball past Tim to score the goal. Now she was standing there glaring at Will while Tim was lying on the ground crying with laughter.

Finally she spoke. "It's time you went home, Tim. It's gone eight. And you can get ready for bed now Will." She turned and marched angrily up the steps.

Tim picked himself up, shrugged his shoulders at Will and set off home on his bike. "Fat lot of good you were," muttered Will. "You could at least have stopped laughing."

He turned into the house with a sigh. As he passed the kitchen he stopped to say, "Sorry, mum," before carrying on upstairs. She turned and looked at him in the way she always did when she was annoyed. Will had learned over the years that it was usually better not to try to explain. That simply prolonged the trouble. It was quicker and simpler to say sorry and then retire to his bedroom looking sad. Once he was in his bedroom he could spend a peaceful hour or so reading his comics and listening to his music. Finally, his mother would come upstairs feeling very guilty that she had been angry at Will and would then invite him to come downstairs and have an extra bottle of Coke and, if he was lucky, a chocolate brownie. These tactics had served him well for a couple of years now and he didn't see why they shouldn't work again.

"I'm sorry about the garden," he said again, and with what he hoped was a miserable and repentant face he plodded his way upstairs.

Once he was safe in his bedroom, he put his music on, lay down on his bed and listened intently for a while before picking up *Tintin in Tibet*. Tintin had just survived terrible danger in the mountains and had arrived at a monastery where he was busy explaining the purpose of his mission to the Grand Abbot when... there was a knock at the door and it was pushed open. As he had predicted, his mother was standing there.

"Would you like to come downstairs for a drink, Will? Chuck's just got back from Tibet and he's brought something I think you might like to see."

Rather reluctantly he closed his book. Most probably he would have to wait for an hour or more to see how Tintin and his friends got on at the monastery.

Downstairs he chose a bottle of Coke and took off the cap carefully. There was a special promotion on at the moment and you could win up to a hundred rupees if that figure was printed on the inside of the cap. He looked. Five rupees. Oh well, it was better than nothing. He turned to his mother.

"Any chocolate brownies?"

"In the tin, I think. Help yourself. To one," she added quickly as she saw the look on Will's face.

He went through into the sitting room and threw himself onto the rather hard and hairy sofa. His father and Chuck were at the other end of the large room talking. For lack of anything better to do, he started to listen. Chuck was speaking. Will liked listening to his American drawl.

"I'll be honest, I thought he was yet another begging kid so I was just about to push him away when I saw this ball of fur in his hand. I was reaching down to take it from him when this Tibetan guy comes charging across the square, yelling at the kid and looking as though he's just about to give him the biggest hiding of his life. But when he sees me he backs off. Apparently the kid had just taken off when his old man had tried to sell the cub to some Chinese trader. I guess the kid saved its life. I didn't know what to do. In the end we negotiated a price and took it away. The question is, what do we do with it now?"

"Do with what?" Will was suddenly on his feet, Coke bottle in one hand, high-fiving Chuck with the other. "What are we going to do with what? The cub?"

Chuck smiled. "I wondered when you'd realise..." He held out his huge hands towards Will. In them was the lynx cub.

For a moment Will said nothing. Then he leaned forward to take the cub. "It's beautiful," was all he could think to say.

There was a pause. His parents looked at one another meaningfully.

Then his father turned to Chuck. "What exactly are you suggesting we do with it?"

"I fly out of here the day after tomorrow. I can't take it with me. Even if I got it through quarantine it wouldn't survive. The lynx is a high altitude animal. Kathmandu is around fifteen hundred metres but it may not survive even at this height. In the wild they don't come much below three thousand metres. It wouldn't have a chance back home. It seems to me like fate took a hand in saving this one. Can you look after it?"

"Yes. Oh please, please, yes!" It was Will who said it but he could tell from his parents' faces that they would have said the same thing. And so it was agreed. The lynx would find a home in Kathmandu until it was old enough and strong enough to be released – if it ever was.

Will picked up the cub and held it tight against his chest. "It can sleep in my room, can't it?" he asked.

Slowly he ascended the stairs. When he was ready for bed, he held the cub in his arms and looked out over the garden. It was full moon and the mountains were clear, their snow glistening in the bright light. He looked up at the stars, so many. He felt strangely happy.

More than five hundred kilometres away, Sonam looked at the same stars, then silently cried himself to sleep.

Chapter Six

When Will woke up the next morning it was barely light. His first thought was for the lynx cub and he put out his hand to feel it and convince himself that the events of the night before were not simply a dream. He felt to the foot of the bed. Nothing. He was fully awake now and afraid. Then he calmed himself and ran his hands carefully around the edges of the bed. The cub was there, squashed between the bed and the wall. When it felt Will pick it up, it opened its eyes wide and stared at him before finally closing them again in sleep.

Will dressed quickly and went downstairs. Nobody else was up and he went out into the garden. He took the cub with him and placed it on the grass to see if it could walk. It took a couple of steps and then stopped. It mewed worriedly and Will picked it up and sat cuddling it, just gazing at the city below as the sun broke through and the world began to wake up. Their house was built on a small hill overlooking the tennis courts that belonged to the American Embassy Club. As he fondled the cub, he gazed absent-mindedly at the empty courts in front of him.

The top of the wire netting that surrounded the courts was home to large numbers of crows. They were everywhere. Will picked one out and followed it as it flapped from side to side. "Almost beautiful," he muttered to himself, looking at the glossy black feathers, "but I hate that big ugly beak." He pulled the cub closer as if to protect it.

There was a small flock of crows inside the wire now, swooping in big circles, landing in groups, cawing noisily. Will's eye was caught by a sparrow that had just flown off the top of the wire and down into the court.

Suddenly all the crows were up and flying. The sparrow seemed to realise the danger it was in and turned to fly low and fast along the netting. But now it was trapped. The pack of crows was closing in on it, it was going to fly into the wire...

Will was on his feet and shouting, "No, no" and grabbing a stone he hurled it towards the court. But it fell far short. The leading crow was now flapping heavily in an attempt to clear the wire and escape the other crows who were cawing loudly, anxious to steal the fluttering sparrow from the leader's beak.

Will was shocked and angry. He held the cub tighter to his chest and went inside. For the rest of the day the incident of the crows and the sparrow hung over him like a bad omen.

Sonam had made a decision. He would go. He would leave his parents and start on the journey that the monk had described. He remembered the monk's words clearly and in truth he had thought of little else since their meeting.

"The place you describe is a long way from here and to reach it you will have to go on a long journey. You will make this journey. It is your fate and no-one escapes that. You are young but I sense this journey will come soon. There will be danger and you will travel much of the way alone. I cannot tell you how but the cub you have saved is in some way part of this. There is something special about you, Sonam, but you will have to find out for yourself what it is. And when you have found it, you must be true to it."

Well, if your fate could not be escaped, there didn't seem to be much point in putting it off.

It was about four in the morning, or so Sonam judged by the dark sky that was streaked with the first signs of morning light. He made his way very quietly out of the tent and stood for a moment. He knew what he was about to do was wrong but he felt he had no choice. He went back inside the tent to where his parents were sleeping soundly. He ran his fingers over his father's jacket until he found the pocket where he kept his money. There were three five dollar notes, several ten dollar notes and three ones. He took the three fives, the money that had been paid for the cub. The others he put back.

His father turned over restlessly and Sonam froze. If his father woke up now, he would surely get the thrashing he had so narrowly escaped the day before. But he need not have worried. His father's eyes remained closed and it would be an hour before he woke up and several more before he realised that the money was missing.

Sonam went outside, called Nima and chained her. Then he took off her collar, threw his arms around her neck and held her tightly for several seconds. There were tears in his eyes when he released her.

"See you Nima," he whispered and he slipped away before her whining could wake anyone up.

Sonam had no real plan. They were camped on the edge of the city and he started to walk towards the centre where he knew there was a truck park. The only means of transport for long distances were the Chinese trucks that travelled the road between Lhasa and the Nepal border. These were few and far between but Sonam knew that if he was to travel that route there was no other way.

After walking for half an hour, he was within sight of the truck park. Although it was barely light he could see people moving about. A group of men was sitting outside a wood and corrugated iron hut drinking early morning tea. They were huddled together, their faces lit by a single bare electric light bulb. They looked cold and miserable.

Sonam stayed in the shadows and crept around to look at the trucks. There were about twenty or thirty of them and they were huge. Although he had often seen them on the roads, they seemed much bigger close up. He slipped in the mud and splashed through the deep puddles. His shoes were now black with a sticky mixture of mud and oil. He peered underneath trucks that were propped up on blocks of wood and once he almost gave himself away when he turned around a corner and nearly stepped on the arm of a man lying stretched out in the mud. He was repairing the truck's suspension and his head was turned away from Sonam. He had been lucky.

After twenty minutes or so, Sonam knew that there were five trucks that looked as though they were leaving that morning, six that could not possibly go anywhere and another dozen or so about which he could tell nothing.

He crept closer to the group of men drinking tea. None of them seemed in any great hurry to move.

Most of their glasses had been refilled and they seemed happy to talk. Sonam understood little of what they said. He knew only a few words of Chinese and in any case they spoke too fast. Finally he concentrated his attention on one of the men. He was tall and he was doing most of the talking. His hands were oil-stained and he gripped his tea in a tight fist. From his movements, Sonam guessed he was getting ready to leave. Finally, he stood up and said something to the others. Sonam caught the words Nepal and Zhangmu. Zhangmu was the border town into Nepal, even Sonam knew that, and effectively there was only one road. His mind was made up. Had the monk not said that the cub was in some way part of his fate? Then he would follow it and see where it took him.

With his heart thumping so loudly that he was sure it could be heard, Sonam followed the man to his truck. He was about to speak to the driver when he realised that there were already other people in the cab. What was he to do? The driver had climbed aboard and the engine was already turning over. He ran to the back of the truck. There was a tarpaulin stretched tight across the load. In growing desperation he pulled at one edge. The truck was starting to move. He took his foot off the ground and balanced for a moment on the step at the back, struggling frantically to shift the tarpaulin aside. Finally it gave and he hauled himself over the tailgate. He heard someone shouting to the driver but it was doubtful if he could hear anything over the roar of the spluttering engine. As the truck gathered speed, Sonam lay still on the hard metal floor, his heart pounding and his breathing loud in his ears. He was on his way to Kathmandu.

Chapter Seven

The truck rattled its way out of the park and onto the streets of Shigatse. Sonam had pulled himself into the back and was sprawled uncomfortably over a pile of pipes, bags of cement and rods of steel. Obviously the truck was taking building materials to Zhangmu. He squirmed around in an attempt to get comfortable but more or less wherever he sat something stuck in his back and forced him into some tortuous position. He didn't know how long the journey would take but a few hours like this, he thought, and he would never walk again!

By now it was getting light and his early morning start, together with the anxiety he had felt at leaving home and searching for a ride, were beginning to tell. Despite his discomfort, Sonam's eyes were closing and he started to doze as the truck left the town and speeded up on the open road. Soon he was sleeping lightly.

He was jerked awake by a thud as they hit a pothole. The whole vehicle lurched wildly to one side and for a moment he thought it was going to turn over. He was thrown forward and he felt his leg scraping the steel before he crashed into one of the bigger pipes. He put his hand up to his head and felt his fingers become sticky with blood. He looked at them in horror. They were covered in a thick mixture of mud, oil and blood. Then he heard a shouted curse from the driver's cab. The truck was pulling to an erratic stop. He heard doors slam and footsteps walking around the side of the truck. All he could do was hold his breath and hope.

This time he was lucky. The footsteps stopped at the side of the truck. Then he heard and felt the thud of steel on steel. What was happening? With more shouting, the driver's door slammed shut, there was a grating of gears and the truck started to move. Sonam breathed freely again. He knew that the wound on his head was not serious and he could feel the blood already beginning to congeal when he touched it. His leg was painful but it was a scrape rather than anything deeper. He struggled to get more comfortable and his eyes closed. It had been a long morning.

He slept for several hours, or so it seemed. When he woke up he was hungry and cold. The engine of the truck was straining and he looked out from under the tarpaulin. At first he wondered where he was. He could see nothing but clouds. The road was twisting and turning and the air was cold and damp. Then the road straightened and he could see through the mist a large pile of rocks by the roadside. The truck slowed to a stop. The doors slammed and through the gap in the tarpaulin Sonam could see the driver and his passengers stretching themselves. Strings of prayer flags were flapping noisily in the wind. One of the passengers went to the pile of stones and added one. They had arrived at the top of one of the two five thousand metre passes that lay between Shigatse and Zhangmu.

For an hour after that they lost height. By this time Sonam's stomach was hurting. He had to have food. He was desperately uncomfortable. His legs ached and his head was beginning to throb. He was losing sight of the danger he was in if anyone found him. He simply had to get out, move around and get something to eat.

When the truck stopped some time later at a roadside cafe, it was torture waiting for the driver and passengers to get out of the cab. The cafe was a wooden shed and the food was cooked on an open fire. He could see the smoke and the flames of the stove inside the hut and smell the frying momos. It was all he could do to stop himself shouting at the passengers to move faster but he kept quiet until they were seated inside and warming themselves by the fire.

As silently as he could, he pulled back the corner of the tarpaulin until there was a gap big enough for him to crawl through. The tailgate of the truck was three or four feet off the ground and he knew he would be very exposed as he climbed over it. But it was a risk he was going to have to take. Very carefully he slipped one leg between the tarpaulin and the tailgate, edged his bottom over the edge... and almost died of fright when he felt himself grabbed by the seat of his trousers, dragged forcibly out of the truck and thrown roughly to the ground.

"So, little thief, I've caught you."

Standing above him, a hand raised to hit him, was the driver.

"I... I wasn't trying to steal anything," said Sonam. "I was just..."

"Oh no?" said the driver. "Not trying to steal anything? What do you take me for? I've seen all these tricks before. What do you think I am? Stupid?"

"But I wasn't," said Sonam. "I wasn't stealing..." He could feel himself close to tears.

"Don't lie to me, you filthy scum," roared the driver. "It happens on almost every trip. As the truck slows down on the hills some brat like you runs along behind and climbs in. Then when the truck gets to wherever it is your friends are waiting, you throw out as much stuff as you can for them to collect. In a few moments half the bags of cement have disappeared. That's happened to a lot of drivers. But it's not going to happen to me you little lout and I'll make sure you never try this trick on any of the other drivers either."

As he was shouting he was pulling a heavy leather belt from his waist. His intention was obvious. He was going to beat Sonam as a warning to all the other thieves who tried to rob trucks.

"No, listen..."

But it was too late. The driver brought the belt crashing down on Sonam, who screamed as he raised his arm to protect his face. The belt was raised again and again and after the first few blows Sonam gave up trying to avoid it and curled himself up into a tight little ball. By this time his screams had brought the truck's passengers and the owner of the cafe rushing out to see what was going on. The owner was a tall, strong-looking woman with a wide face and thick black hair plaited into a bun at the back of her head. Her face was usually kind and her eyes smiling but now she was angry.

"Leave the boy alone. What has he done? Leave him!"

She started to shout at the driver but the act of beating Sonam seemed to have made him angrier still. He lashed at him again with the belt and then landed a vicious kick on his chest. Sonam rolled over and over in pain, his hands gripping his stomach. This was too much for the passengers. They struggled to drag the driver into the hut and take the belt from him, where they gave him sweet tea and brandy in an effort to calm him down. Sonam, they ignored. Thieves deserved what they got and, besides, if they angered the driver they would not get to Zhangmu that night.

Sonam was sobbing. His head hurt, his chest ached and he was sure one of his ribs was broken. He tried to sit up but the pain in his side was unbearable. He felt his face with his fingers; one of his eyes was swollen and tender; there was blood on his cheek. His nose was running and the tears streaked his face grey.

He watched the passengers get back into the truck. As the driver walked past Sonam, he spat into the dust but he did not touch him again. The tea and brandy had done their work. The truck drove off leaving a cloud of dust hanging in the air.

After a few minutes the owner of cafe came out. "My name is Tsering," she said, "and yours is...?"

"Sonam."

"Well, Sonam, even if you are a little thief you don't deserve to be beaten by a pig of a lorry driver," and she took him into the hut and sat him down by the fire while she went to get water to clean him up. He gasped in pain as she washed his face and she was shocked at the bruises on his ribs from where the kicks had landed. But soon he was warmer and more comfortable and she told him to lie on the wooden bench next to the fire while she fried some momos for him. As she did so, she talked.

"He's a nasty one that driver. Gao they call him. They all stop here, the drivers, the tourists as well. There's nowhere else to get food or drink. He does this run a couple of times a month. He drinks brandy all day and it makes him bad tempered. It's not an easy life, heaven knows, driving a truck in a country like this but that doesn't give him the right to do what he did to you. Mind you, you shouldn't have been stealing, so you've only got yourself to blame."

"I wasn't," said Sonam. And, as best he could, he told her why he was trying to get to Kathmandu and how he had hidden in the back of the truck. When he had finished his story she just smiled at him and he couldn't tell whether she believed him or not. After he had eaten his noodle soup and a large plate of fried momos, he found that he didn't very much care and it was only a matter of minutes before he was deeply asleep. As he closed his eyes, he saw the broad face of Tsering smiling down at him.

The Landcruiser that pulled up outside the cafe two hours later was similar to the one that had taken the lynx cub off to Kathmandu and when he awoke to the sound of the engine outside, Sonam thought for a moment that he was back in the square at Shigatse. But only for a moment. He was quickly awake and tried to scramble off the bench to let the visitors sit down. Involuntarily, he cried out in pain. There was no way he could move, let alone stand up.

There were five people, two Italians, two Americans and one man who was talking to Tsering in Tibetan. He was certainly not Tibetan though. He was greeting Tsering as though she were an old friend – as indeed she was. Mike had done this trip a couple of dozen times. At that moment he was asking

Tsering about the boy. "So who's the kid? One of your sister's? He doesn't look too good, is he OK?"

"I don't know who he is, Mike. Can you look at him? He said that he stowed away in the truck to try to get to Kathmandu. The driver said he was stealing and beat him up. Badly. I'm not sure of the truth. Oh, and there's a lynx cub and a monk mixed up in this somewhere as well. Sounds just your kind of thing." She grinned. It was a good story and Mike was a sucker for good stories.

He went across to look at Sonam. The boy was a pitiful sight even though Tsering had cleaned him up. His right eye was bruised and swollen so much that it was half-closed. There was a seeping cut on his left cheek. His left arm, with which he had tried to shield himself, was blue from the elbow to his hand. When Mike went to unbutton his shirt, Sonam gasped in pain.

"OK boy, I'm not going to hurt you. But I need to see what's wrong and then we can decide what to do about it. Easy does it."

It was impossible to tell without an x-ray whether or not the rib was broken but the bruising made it clear that he had been kicked hard. Mike stripped Sonam to the waist and with the help of one of the others began to bind up his chest. Mike could not tell how much real damage had been done but the boy had certainly been knocked around very badly. More worryingly, his forehead was burning and it looked very much as though Sonam would soon be running a fever. The boy needed food, warmth, shelter and plenty to drink. Had there been a nearby hospital, he would have benefited from that as well. But there wasn't. At four and a half thousand metres on one of the bleakest roads in Asia you were pretty much on your own.

"What is your name? Where are you going?" asked Mike. His accent was a bit funny but Sonam understood. So he told his story again, almost word for word. This time he was believed.

He watched anxiously as Mike and Tsering talked about him. "I can take him in three days' time. I should be back from Lhasa by then. That'll also give him time to recover. But it's risky. He'll get into really bad trouble if the Chinese at the border get him." Mike was clearly worried but in the end he agreed to take the boy with him as far as the border. He couldn't take the risk of smuggling him across it illegally. But if Sonam could manage to cross on his own, Mike would take him on to Kathmandu.

Chapter Eight

When Will got back home from school that evening he rushed straight through the front door to see the cub. He knew from his mother's long face that something was wrong.

"Where is he? Where's the cub?"

"Will, I'm sorry. I don't think the cub is going to survive. He's suddenly started to drag himself around. He doesn't seem able to use his back legs at all."

"What happened?"

"I don't know. He might have fallen down the stairs sometime during the day. But I'm not sure. He had free run of the house. When I came back home I found him lying on the rug outside the kitchen. He looked up at me and then started to drag himself along using only his front legs. Come on, I'll show you."

She led the way into the living room where the cub was now sitting upright in a cardboard box. She picked him up carefully and set him down gently onto his back legs, seeing if they could take any weight. There was no response. It was obvious that the back legs were completely paralysed.

"What do we do now?" Will was looking completely downcast.

"We wait for your father to come. I phoned him at work and told him what had happened. He said he'd ask around and see who we could contact. Someone around here must know something about lynxes. Now you stay with him and I'll bring you a drink in a minute. How was school?"

"OK."

Will sat down by the cub's side. He picked it up a few times to see if it could take any weight on its back legs but each time the result was just the same. There was no strength there at all. Will knew that all the power of a cat is concentrated in the hind legs. If they remained paralysed there would never be any possibility of the cub eventually being released into the wild.

He heard the front door open and then the sound of his mother and father talking in the kitchen. After a few moments his father came into the room.

"Hi, Will, let's have a look at this cub." He repeated what Will had just done and came to the same conclusion. "I don't think he's broken anything but I can't be sure. We need some x-rays first. I've been in touch with the zoo vet and he says he'll help. In fact he's probably waiting for us now. Put the cub in its box and let's go."

As they drove across the city, his father told Will what he had done. "I've had everyone in the office running around like headless chickens. We've been telephoning anyone who might know anything and, as it turned out, a lot of people who knew nothing. It appears that there aren't too many people around who know anything about *Lynx isabellina*, to give him his proper name. For a start, there aren't many of them in captivity." He swerved to avoid a cow crossing the road. "A couple of zoos in America have them but most of the real interest in Himalayan cats is concentrated on the snow leopard. Everyone knows the lynx exists and you can see a dozen Tibetans wearing lynx fur hats on any cold day of the year. But there's a distinct lack of hard information about what you do to try and rear a live one. We could be in the history books if we succeed. Anyway," he paused to blast his horn at a pedestrian who was walking his goat down the middle of the road, "I emailed London Zoo as well, just in case anyone there knows anything."

They were approaching the zoo by this time. The animals were housed in a rather run down series of low concrete buildings but most of the ones they passed on the way to the veterinary unit looked healthy enough. The zoo vet was kind and helpful. He ran his fingers over all of the lynx's joints and explored his back with patience and considerable care. It was not, he thought, broken but the x-rays would show exactly what was happening.

"Is he OK?" Will couldn't stop himself from asking the question.

The vet looked at the boy's worried face. He wanted to say yes but in all honesty he couldn't do so.

"I really can't say. I hope so. I would like him to be and so would you. But there are many problems about rearing animals in captivity. Even when we know a lot about the animal – about its diet, its habitat, the diseases it suffers from – even when we know all about these things we sometimes cannot save the animal. In the case of the lynx," he shrugged, "there is so much we do not even know. All we can do is try."

They had to wait a short time for the x-ray but finally the vet pinned it up over the light box on the wall. He studied it carefully for a few minutes and Will looked at it intently too, although he was largely trying to sort out which bit of the animal was which. The vet started to trace his finger along the main bones.

"Well, the first news is good news. There is no break or fracture of the spine. The bones of the legs are also whole. But many of these bones look smaller and more frail than they should. It must be diet. If the bones stay as thin as this they will break very easily. But I cannot help you much more than this. You say you have emailed London Zoo. They are geared up for research and even if they do not have a resident expert they will soon get in touch with someone who is. In the meantime, feed him, care for him and hope for the best. But I can tell you nothing is broken. To tell you more than that I would need to do blood tests. I'm sorry but at the moment that is just not possible."

Will and his father left the zoo a little happier than they had arrived. It was a relief to know that his spine was not damaged. If it had been, the cub would certainly have died. Possibly they would have had to put him down. That was one decision his father was glad he did not to have to make.

It was supper time when they reached home again and over the meal the family started on its favourite topic again – what to call the cub. This had been going on for a couple of days now but they had barely got past the stage of calling the cub "it". At first this had been because they couldn't work out whether it was male or female. They had resolved that one now – it was male.

"He came from Tibet, so it should be something Tibetan," said Jill. "What about Lung-Ta, the Wind Horse? That's a beautiful name. How about it, Steve?" Her husband hesitated and Will jumped in.

"He's not a horse. Let's call him something fierce like Tiger."

"It's a beer," said Steve. "We can't have him called after a beer."

"Tashi, then," said Jill. "It's short, easy to remember, has a distinctive sound and it means 'good fortune' or 'auspiciousness'. This cub has had plenty of good fortune already and his arrival has been auspicious for us. Isn't that right, Tashi?"

As if on cue the cub looked up from his basket at the side of the table.

That was taken as an auspicious sign and the conversation moved on to the paralysis.

"The vet was really helpful," Steve was saying, "but apart from establishing that there are no broken bones, we're not actually any wiser than we were before. If the bones are weak we need to build them up. I don't know about lynxes but when I was at school we were always being told to drink milk. My mum always said I had to drink milk to get strong teeth and bones. It's the calcium. So maybe that's what we should do – give Tashi some milk with added calcium."

"OK, we can try it. And maybe we can add some bonemeal. That's calcium rich. It grows good vegetables so maybe it will grow good lynxes as well." Jill grinned as she got up to clear away the plates. "Come on, Will, help me wash up. Then we'll get down to some serious feeding."

Feeding Tashi was more of a problem than they had imagined. He did not seem particularly hungry at first but, with a bit of coaxing and persuading, he ate some pieces of minced buffalo meat Jill had bought from the butcher's stall at the corner of their lane and lightly cooked. They mixed some extra bonemeal in with it and were pleased when the cub finally ate a reasonable amount. Tashi also proved willing to drink milk in whatever quantities it was offered.

"Well done," Will whispered to the cub when the meal was over. "You keep eating like this and you'll grow up to be big and strong, just like me!" He cuffed the cub playfully around the ear and settled down to play with Tashi who seemed to have gained energy from the food. Although he could not use his back legs at all, he could still move around surprisingly nimbly using his front legs. He held himself up on them and dragged his back legs along behind.

The cub was now about the same size as a small cat and he seemed very happy to behave in much the same sort of way. Will soon had him chasing a piece of string all over the floor and he had to be rescued as he got stuck behind cupboards and trapped under rugs. Being so young, he tired quickly and bedtime for the boy and the cub arrived at more or less the same time.

"Can I take him up with me?" Will asked.

His mother hesitated. She looked across at Steve. "Is it alright?"

He nodded his head. "Let him for tonight, Jill. But don't count on it every night, Will."

With a shout of delight Will picked up the cub, ready to take him upstairs. Tashi was already asleep as he laid him carefully on the bed. "Good night little lynx," he said. "Sleep well and sweet dreams."

For a long time Will did not go to sleep. He sat and gazed at the sleeping cub, watching his fur stretch and retract under his fingers as he stroked it. He ran his hands over the useless back legs and prayed in his heart that some use would return to them. The cub slept on, unaware of the boy's hopes and fears. After a while, Will snuggled under his quilt and lay thinking about the life that Tashi must have led until then. He imagined the brutal man who had killed his mother. How could anyone kill a creature as beautiful as this? He began to drift off to sleep. In those early dreams the cub grew big and strong and roamed the walled garden so that visitors were afraid to enter. But to Will he was always gentle and obedient. One drizzly day he put him on a lead and walked him through the streets of Kathmandu and everyone stopped and stared at the boy and his strange pet. No, not pet. Nothing so proud and independent could be a pet...

Finally, as sleep took a deeper hold, he dreamed of a forest with tall trees. Through the forest ran a stream, white water cascading down over the boulders and fallen branches. The undergrowth was dense but if you pushed it aside you came eventually to a clearing. At first the clearing looked empty but if you looked hard enough you could see a lynx, its head turning back to look over its shoulder before it disappeared amongst the trees.

Chapter Nine

When Steve got back to the office after lunch two days later, there was an email waiting for him from London Zoo. His delight at getting an expert response so quickly soon turned to alarm as he read it:

Dear Steve,
Thanks for your mail. I'm not sure I am an expert but I'll certainly help in any way that I can!
The paralysis of the back legs you describe is not uncommon and we think about 10% of cubs in the wild die because of it. The problem starts in the back legs but it can spread. There is a general softening of the bones and they fracture very easily. If the jaw is fractured, the cub can die of starvation.
The solution is to change its diet. You don't say much in your mail about what you are feeding him but if it is largely red meat then that could be the cause of the problem. Odd though it may sound, too much calcium can do the damage. There is also the possibility of infection through bad meat. A proper diet for him would be a whole chicken a day or a small goat carcass every three days. When I say a whole

chicken, I mean just that – feathers, beak, guts, the lot! It's essential for a balanced diet. If you feed him goat, include the skin and guts. You should also give him some cod liver oil and some vitamin A. Some bonemeal is fine if you can get it.
If, as I suspect, the problem is too much calcium, then you need to inject phosphorous to balance it out. Your local vet should help. It should be injected into the neck. You should see a pretty rapid improvement if this is the cause of the problem. I'll be interested to know what happens. Can you mail me in a week?
Good luck. I really do hope it works.
Simon Goodfield

Steve sat back from the screen, took a deep breath, pressed print and then re-read the mail carefully. They had done everything wrong. For somebody normally so calm he almost panicked. Picking up his mobile, he phoned Jill.

"Hi, it's Steve. Look, I've got a mail from London Zoo. Don't feed Tashi anything until I get home. Anything at all, OK? I'm coming now. Work will have to manage without me for a bit this afternoon. We've done just about everything wrong that we could have done."

He didn't wait for Jill's reply but grabbed his coat and left the building at a half run.

Ten minutes later she was reading the printout.

"Steve, this is terrible. Not only weren't we doing anything useful, we may have been doing actual damage. Let's hope it's not too late."

It was not long before their horror turned into practical arrangements. Steve would ring the zoo vet again and organise the phosphorous injections. He would also get the cod liver oil and the vitamin A. Jill would get the chicken. She shuddered at the thought of it with its head and feathers still on but at least getting hold of one here would be a great deal easier than it would have been in England. In Kathmandu, the chickens sat outside the butchers' shops in cages, waiting for someone to choose them for supper.

On her way up the lane, she remembered with some amusement how squeamish they had all been when they had arrived from England. Will had only been six. A friend had taken them for a walk through the old part of the city. By accident they had ended up in a narrow lane in which there were a series of butchers' stalls. Will had yelled in disgust as he found himself staring at the head of a goat on a butcher's slab about two feet away and exactly at his eye level. Now he wouldn't even look twice. She wasn't sure whether this was good or bad. Were they becoming more tolerant or less sensitive?

When she got back with a chicken stuffed head first into a polythene bag and its feet sticking out of the top, Steve was just about to put Tashi in his carry box and take him to see the vet.

"Can't you wait for Will? He'll be so disappointed if you go without him. He'll be back from school soon. He's really attached to Tashi. You should take him if you can."

"Alright. I don't suppose a few minutes will make much difference. Give me the chicken and I'll cut it up."

He hacked it roughly into four pieces and then put them into the fridge. It was not long before Will came bursting through the front door. He didn't even have time to take off his coat.

"Come on, we're going to take Tashi to the vet again. I'll tell you the whole story on the way."

Will dashed into the kitchen to grab a brownie and then, with a cheeky grin back at his mum, joined his dad and Tashi in the car. Steve told him about the mail and the changes they would be making to Tashi's diet.

"He also needs injections of phosphorous, which is why we are going to the zoo. I need to get some and to see how the injections are done. The neck is a pretty sensitive area and I want to see exactly where the needle goes in. If I get that wrong it could do a lot of damage." He hesitated, then decided to carry on. "When I spoke to Mr Sharma on the phone, he suggested we try acupuncture as well."

"What's that?"

"An old Chinese form of medicine. They stick tiny needles into the neural pathways. But we're almost there so Mr Sharma can tell you himself."

The vet was pleased to see them and as charming as ever. He said he had been studying the x-rays again but had come to the same conclusion: nothing was broken and nothing was badly damaged. Steve showed him the printout which he read with great interest. He looked up at them both a little sadly.

"In the West, it's so good. You have money for research and you have an expert for this and an expert for that. I have visited these zoos and the facilities are wonderful. Also, communications are so much better than they are here. If you have something you don't know how to treat, you can phone or email someone for advice. Whereas here," he shrugged, "there is only me. And I have a whole zoo to care for. Still, let's see how Tashi is today."

He put the cub down carefully on the examination table and again felt the back legs, hoping there would be some response. But there was nothing. The legs were still completely paralysed.

"On several occasions," he said, "I have tried acupuncture on cases of paralysis. Sometimes by passing a small electric current through the muscle it is possible to stimulate it into life. Acupuncture also helps the natural healing energies of the body. I will inject the phosphorous and then, with your permission, I should like to try it."

"How many times have you done it before?"

"About eight, I think. In every case it proved effective. There was a monkey which had not moved its arm for a month; after a few sessions of treatment it made rapid progress. You need not worry; there is no risk. It will work or it won't but no harm will come to Tashi if it doesn't." He turned to Will. "Have you ever broken your leg?"

Will shook his head.

"If your leg is in plaster for ages it is often difficult to get the muscles working again. It seems that the brain cannot find them after such a long time of being unable to move. Perhaps Tashi's brain has forgotten how to move the muscles in his back legs. The acupuncture may remind him".

While he had been talking, the vet had prepared the injection of phosphorous. He showed Steve exactly how it should be given.

"Do not be frightened by it. If you inject as I have demonstrated, you will do no harm and the phosphorous itself may do a great deal of good."

When the injection was completed, he looked enquiringly at Steve and Will. "Well, have you decided? Do we try acupuncture?"

"It seems to me we have nothing to lose," Steve answered. Will nodded.

The cub was laid carefully on the table again and Will and his father were asked to hold him as still as they could. The acupuncture needles were very long and very thin. The vet inserted two into the hind legs and then moved them around trying, as he explained, to make the energy flow. There was no response. Then he attached clips to the top of the needles. "I am going to run a small electric current through the muscle," he said. "We will see if that produces any response."

And astonishingly it did. Suddenly the legs jerked and twitched into life in a most unnatural way but at least it proved that they could still move. The vet was smiling. By increasing the current very slightly the limbs moved more vigorously.

"Perhaps," he said at last, "perhaps you and Tashi will be lucky. I have some hope now."

The car journey home was very different from the one to the zoo. Both Steve and Will were full of optimism. Somehow, just seeing the legs move had encouraged them. They had agreed to take the cub back over the next few days for further treatment. If the acupuncture worked and the change of diet was effective, it looked as though Tashi might be back to normal within a week.

Jill was waiting impatiently when they returned. "Come on you lot, I want to see how Tashi handles the chicken."

They went into the garden, Will carrying the dribbling quarter chicken in his hand. It dripped on the path in gobs of bloody fluid. He teased the cub with it, swinging it just over Tashi's head and brushing his nose with the feathers. The cub tried to catch it with one paw but without the use of his hind legs he soon over-balanced and rolled onto his back.

Then Will tickled his tummy with the feathers and the cub tried again to catch his prey as Will whisked it suddenly out of reach. Finally, he took pity on Tashi and threw the chicken into the air. It landed with a thud. The cub approached it and sniffed carefully. Then he hit it, first with one paw and then with the other. For several seconds he batted the chicken from one side to the other before sinking his teeth into the mound of feathers. Will watched fascinated as he growled and gnawed at the increasingly messy heap on the ground and found it difficult not to laugh when Tashi looked up at him, several fine feathers stuck ridiculously on the end of his nose.

Chapter Ten

Sonam had started to run a fever very shortly after Mike left for Lhasa. Mike had said that he would be back in three or four days when he had shown the tourists around and had told Tsering to get the boy fit for the journey to Zhangmu. After that, if Sonam could cross the border on his own, he would meet him on the other side and take him on to Kathmandu.

For several hours after Mike left, Sonam had slept by the fire. He was so still that Tsering had started to wonder if he was seriously ill. When she had time away from the customers she sat with him, stroking his hair and feeling his forehead to gauge his temperature. He was hot, at times burningly so, but she could do nothing other than be with him and try to calm him. It was obvious that his fever was making him hallucinate and from time to time he cried out in his sleep. At one point he had rambled on for several minutes.

But this morning he was suddenly looking better. He had woken early and looked around him, seeing the hut and the fire as if for the first time. He saw Tsering making dough but wasn't sure that he recognised her. She was not his mother, that was certain – so who was she?

At that moment she turned to look at him. "Sonam, you're awake. How are you feeling?"

He looked at her rather blankly and then smiled. "I'm OK. Where am I?"

"You don't know? Well, you're a few hundred metres from the Lagpa-la pass. You've been sick. Take it easy and I'll bring you some tea."

She filled a glass with some tea and brought it over. She put her arm around his shoulders. "You really don't remember anything? Not the truck driver, or Mike, or anything?"

Slowly she told him what had happened and, as she told him, he began to remember for himself. The only things of which he had no memory at all were Mike's departure and the days that had followed.

"You were running a fever. You were talking in your sleep and shouting out!"

"What did I say?"

"I don't remember much of it. You were obviously very frightened at one point because you yelled, 'Don't... Don't... I had to do it, I had to.' Other times you seemed to be dreaming a lot about this lynx cub of yours. You didn't make a lot of sense. I remember you saying something like, 'Take good care of him... Can he walk? Why doesn't he move properly? You haven't killed him, have you? You can't have done that. He wasn't saved so you could do that to him.' That dream seemed to go on for a long time. After shouting out something I couldn't understand, you got up from your bed and tried to get out of the door. I stopped you just in time. It was night time and snowing. If you'd gone out then, you would have been lost in the blizzard and I doubt you would ever have come back."

She hugged Sonam closer to her at the thought before getting up to carry on with the cooking. "You've been really sick, Sonam. Now you need to take some rest and get some strength back."

"When does Mike come back?"

"Mike went off to Lhasa. He'll be back here today or tomorrow." She suddenly looked serious. "Sonam, I'm really not sure you are well enough to go with him."

But Sonam shook his head. "I'll be ready. I have to be. It's the only hope I have of getting all the way to Nepal."

And Sonam recovered remarkably quickly as the day went on. At first he simply lay by the fire but, as Tsering's customers started to arrive, he helped her to make the flasks of tea and to prepare vegetables for the fried rice and momos that seemed to be their favourites. Only once did he hide and that was when a Chinese truck pulled up outside. For a few moments he had panicked that somehow Gao had come back to get him. But of course it wasn't Gao, who by then must have driven to the border and been safely back in Shigatse. Still, he shivered to think that while he was sweating with his fever Gao must have passed the door.

Tsering was pleased to see that Sonam's appetite was returning, for in the days of his illness he had eaten very little and she knew that he must be very weak. Today he was eating steadily. His eyes had lost their glassy look and he generally looked healthier. But she was still worried about him. He was better, yes, but he was not really in any state to travel.

Mike finally arrived at about four o'clock. He was alone except for his driver. He had left his group in Lhasa and was returning to Kathmandu overland while they flew back over the Himalayas for one of the world's most spectacular views. He was tired but pleased to see Tsering and Sonam.

"How have you been? Are you ready for the border?"

He went to sit down next to Sonam but Tsering took him to one side.

"Mike, Sonam has been sick almost from the time you left. He's made a good recovery but today is the first day he's been up since you left. I really don't think he's fit enough to go. Can you give him two more days to recover?"

Mike shook his head. "I can't do it. For a start I have to be back in Kathmandu tomorrow. This driver won't wait because he has other people to meet in Zhangmu. I'm being met on the Nepalese side of the border tomorrow morning. All the arrangements have been made. If he's going to come with me, he has to come now."

Tsering looked at him and saw that he would not change his mind. Sonam would have to decide for himself. Mike went across to him.

"Sonam, I have to go now. I know you haven't been well and if you want to stay here for a few days that's fine. Tsering will look after you. But if you want to come with me, we have to go."

Sonam gathered his few things and went across to Tsering. He hugged her hard. "I will come back to see you," he said. "I don't think I'll be long in Kathmandu but I know I have got to go there." He sounded very solemn suddenly.

Tsering watched as he and Mike got into the Landcruiser and set off down the road. The hut would be empty without him.

Mike and Sonam lost no time in planning the rest of the day. Zhangmu was only a few hours' drive but, by the time they got there, it would be dark and so Sonam would not be able to see the country that he would have to cross. He needed to get over the border at night to avoid the guards but, if he was to have any chance of success, he would need a very clear picture in his head of what he was trying to do.

"Have you ever been to Zhangmu, Sonam?" He shook his head. "Then listen to me very carefully. The town is on the side of the mountain about nine kilometres inside the border – at least, it's about nine kilometres if you go by the road. The actual border is the river that runs through a very steep gorge. There are thick forests leading down to the river and they would give you good cover if you tried to go that way. The big problem is that you have to get around the Customs checkpoint at Zhangmu. There's a barrier across the road and it's heavily guarded. Once you get across the check line, there's the nine kilometres of road I told you about before you get down to the river. There's a bridge there called the Friendship Bridge. Once you are across that, you are in Nepal."

Mike paused to give Sonam time to picture the town. Then he started to describe how Sonam might try to avoid the guards.

"If you come to Zhangmu with me, you could try to get down to the river from the town. There is a real risk of you being seen though. There are something like three hundred soldiers stationed there and they can't all be on the border at the same time. Some of them will be patrolling the forests. If you can get down to the river and follow it through the gorge, you might get under the bridge at night and get past the guards that way. Think about it, Sonam, and so will I. You can sleep for an hour or so before we begin the descent to the town. Then we'll have to decide."

Sonam slept but Mike stayed awake, imagining the problems Sonam might have. The boy was better but he was not yet strong and this route meant going down a thousand feet and walking for perhaps two or three kilometres over very rough ground. It would be dangerous, too, especially down in the river gorge where the rocks would be slippery with spray. The more he thought about it, the less possible it seemed.

It was not long before the car started down the series of hairpin bends that would eventually take them through the middle of Zhangmu. The sharp corners threw them together on the back seat and when Sonam woke his head was on Mike's lap. Mike pushed him gently upright.

"Wake up, Sonam, we're nearly there." But Sonam was still sleepy and it was some minutes before he could concentrate on what Mike was saying to him. By then he could see the lights of Zhangmu several hundred feet below. Staring out of the window into the blackness, Sonam could see no sign of the river far below but he could tell by the steepness of the land that it must be a long way below them. And at that moment it suddenly seemed that there was no choice. Sonam would have to go into the heart of the town and then make his way down to the border from there. If the soldiers caught him, well, they caught him. But when Sonam slipped out of the car at the first crossroads, he had no intention of letting that happen.

Chapter Eleven

As animals discovered a very long time ago, looking the same as your surroundings is a very effective means of disguise if you want to avoid getting caught. When Sonam slipped out of the Landcruiser, it was only the vehicle that the locals looked at and he himself had blended into the rest of Zhangmu in seconds. He was just another scruffy Tibetan kid walking the street with all the others. In another town the locals would have realised immediately that he was a stranger. But Zhangmu had a constantly changing population from the trade that went on across the border.

Sonam was starving. He had eaten nothing since setting off with Mike and his fever had left him hungry. Mike had given him a handful of yuan, the Chinese currency, to get food and some Nepalese rupees in case he managed to cross the border in good time. He went into one of the tiny restaurants that clung hazardously to the side of the mountain, built out on stilts over an almost vertical drop to the river below. He ordered rice and chicken.

"Can you pay for it?" The owner had taken one look at him and assumed at first that he was a beggar but when Sonam took out his money he was friendly enough. He was Chinese but he had learnt a little Tibetan.

"So what brings you here? I haven't seen you here before."

Sonam hesitated. "Oh," he said, "I have to buy some things for my parents. They are up in the hills back towards Shigatse. They weren't able to come themselves." By now he was blushing at the string of lies but he couldn't stop once he had started. Some people become silent when they are scared; some talk too much. Sonam carried on. "My mother is sick. My father stayed to take care of her and look after the sheep." The owner looked at him oddly. Even to him this sounded unlikely. The nearest open grazing was too far away for a boy like Sonam to be sent on a shopping trip. Still, it wasn't his business.

The chicken and rice that Sonam had ordered were being cooked in the same room as the eating area. The owner and his family obviously worked and slept in the same place. Their bed was just visible past a torn curtain. Sonam settled in his chair. This was the last food and the last rest he would get until he was safely across the border. The thought filled him with excitement but also fear. The journey through the forest did not worry him too much although he hoped that all the forest demons would be asleep. But the hillside was much steeper than he had imagined and the roar of the river was loud even though it was far, far below. And then there were the border guards.

At that moment there was the sound of well-heeled boots stamping on the ground outside and coming up the steps. Even if he had wanted to, there was nowhere for Sonam to hide from the green uniform that appeared suddenly in the doorway. But the soldier seemed not to notice Sonam as he sat down at the table nearest the window and ordered tea. Soon he and the owner were in deep conversation. It was as well for Sonam's nerves that he did not know what they were saying.

"So, comrade, anything to report?" The soldier was looking hard at the man in front of him. This was part of the round he did every evening and by the time he had finished it there was not much he did not know about what had happened in Zhangmu during the day.

"There is nothing to report, comrade." The owner looked around his empty restaurant. "As you can see, no one is here except the kid over there. And he won't give me much profit!" He laughed aloud.

"Who is the brat?"

Sonam saw the men turn to look at him but he could not hear what they were saying and they were in any case speaking far too fast for him to pick up anything in a language that was alien to him. The owner paused just for a second. Although he did not believe Sonam's story he had no wish to get him into trouble. If he told the guard what he really thought, the boy would be taken to the border post and interrogated in some back room. He might even be beaten – it depended on who was on duty. The guards took no chances with strangers, even children. Children had been used to spy in the past.

"Oh, just some kid. He's been around before. He's harmless. His parents are somewhere on the edge of the town, probably getting drunk with their friends. He must have made a few yuan portering and decided to give himself a decent meal rather than hand over the money for his father to gamble away."

The guard grunted. He finished his cup of tea and went out without paying for it.

Sonam relaxed a little and finished his chicken rice. He should go. He could sense that it was dangerous to linger. He stood up and handed over the money for the food. As he was about to leave, he turned to the owner and grinned. "I need a toilet. Can I go out the back?" The owner shrugged and pointed at the back door. The open hillside at the back of the hut served as a toilet and general rubbish dump. He was surprised when Sonam did not reappear after five minutes but by then he had other customers and had soon forgotten all about him.

As soon as he was outside, Sonam started on the descent to the river. The first section of ground was open scrub made even more treacherous by the waste and rubbish that had been thrown onto it from the huts above. He kept looking anxiously over his shoulder because there was no cover here and if anyone looked out from the houses he would be easily seen. He kept as low to the ground as he could and worked his way down.

He was relieved to reach the trees. Once he was in the woods he felt safer. Now he had only his own fears to cope with. Sonam was used to being out at night but that was usually in the open and he found the trees that now surrounded him claustrophobic and threatening. The leaves and branches overhead cut out nearly all of the light from the moon and the stars and it was not long before he was feeling his way almost entirely by touch. He stretched his arms out ahead of him and tried to push aside the low branches but time and again they whipped back and hit his arms and face. He dropped to a crouch and started to edge down more carefully, leading with his feet. This worked better and he started to make quicker progress, although he slipped and slithered repeatedly. He was covered in cuts and scratches but he had to keep going if there was to be any chance of meeting up with Mike by morning.

All of this time the sound of the river had been growing louder. The fact that he could not see it made it even more frightening for its roar cut out all other sounds. He could not hear the cracking of twigs and rustling of leaves that would warn him of the presence of other creatures, human or animal. All he could do was keep going and hope.

Sonam reckoned that he had been walking, if you could call it that, for about an hour when he sat down to rest. He was exhausted already and he knew that he still had a long way to go. He was thankful that he had eaten or he would have completely run out of energy by now. He slumped down miserably against a tree trunk. He had worked out his plan. He wanted to reach the river that night. Then he would sleep until first light. To attempt to walk across or swim that torrent in darkness would be to risk certain death. He might just as well throw himself straight off the cliff and be done with it.

He pushed on down. He was beginning to lose his footing more frequently. Once he almost cried out loud when his feet suddenly slipped from under him and he found himself falling. He landed with a thump in the tangle of branches of a rhododendron bush. One broken branch stuck painfully into the small of his back and he wasted both time and energy trying to unhook his clothes. By now he was tiring rapidly and he had to drag himself to his feet. The roar of the water was suddenly much closer and when he reached slightly more open ground he could feel flecks of spray on his face. Here he could rest. He was asleep the moment he closed his eyes.

When first light came, Sonam felt as though he had hardly slept at all. The ground had been hard against his already aching body and he was hungry. He stretched, stood up and looked at the river. He was alarmed to see that it was still about a hundred feet below him. He looked down in horror at where he had been sleeping – if he had turned over once too often in the night he would have fallen. It was an almost vertical drop to the water and he had been sleeping on a ledge no more than two metres wide. He judged it to be about six o'clock by the position of the sun. If he was correct, he had just three hours to get across the border and meet Mike.

He set off down the cliff face. His chest was painful as he stretched his arm up to get a good handhold. Then he searched for a knob of rock to put his foot on. Slowly he edged his way down, looking for toeholds and handholds that could take his weight. There were useful creepers and small tree trunks that offered him support and occasionally he was able to pause for breath when the ledges were sufficiently wide for him to stand in comfort. He was making good progress when everything came to a stop. He was some twenty feet above the water on an outcrop of rock and when he looked down Sonam saw that it was completely smooth. There was no way he could climb down it.

He stood looking down at the water and back up at the face he had just come down. Neither upstream nor downstream seemed any better. At this point the river had simply carved its way through the rock. A terrible truth was beginning to become obvious to him. There was no way he could go back the way he had come. He didn't have the strength to climb the cliff again. Turning around he stared at the river below him. Dare he? Dare he jump?

Below the outcrop, the biggish pool was at least fairly calm and it looked deep. Besides, there was no alternative. He jumped.

He hit the water hard. Instead of landing in the top end of the pool he found himself towards the bottom end where the river was already picking up speed as it swirled on downstream. The mountain water was bitingly cold and he gasped at the shock. His lungs filled with water and he stayed under for what seemed like minutes. When he eventually surfaced he had been swept many metres downstream. Slowly he managed to swim towards the opposite bank. Choking and spluttering, he clambered onto it and looked back. It seemed incredible to him that he was still alive. For a few minutes he just sat there shaking, muttering his mantra in prayer, thanking the spirit protector of his family for looking after him.

When he had recovered his breath, he looked downstream. He could see the road bridge quite clearly and he was now much closer than he thought. Even better, the bank between him and the bridge was comparatively flat and well covered by trees. Only at the actual bridge itself was there a danger of him being seen. But surely then he could run for it?

He made good progress until he was within about fifty metres of the bridge. Then he sat down to watch. There were four guards. Two of them watched the road barrier. Of the remaining two, one remained stationary at one end of the bridge while the other marched up and down it, looking over its sides at varying intervals. Sometimes he would be joined by another guard. All the undergrowth had been cleared from both sides of the river and, whatever Sonam did, he knew he would be exposed as he crossed the actual border. All the more reason for doing it as fast as possible. Why would the guards be interested in a boy like him? He was ready to risk it.

Sonam timed it well. He waited until a large bus of tourists was about to cross the bridge before making his move. As he had thought, the guards were more interested in them than in watching the river bed. The bus was held up at the barrier, packets of cigarettes exchanged, greetings shouted. Sonam ran for the bridge. If he could get underneath it, he would be safe. He scrambled along the river bank as fast as he could, slipping on the gravelly path and once he almost fell into the water but he kept his balance and ran on. Twenty yards to go. He had his eyes fixed on the stone pillar in front of him. Ten yards. Then suddenly he was sprawling in the dust. He had gone flying over the outstretched foot of a guard. The river was patrolled after all.

The guard was shouting at him. Frantically Sonam got to his feet and ducked the outstretched arm. He started running. He had a few metres start and surely the gods could not desert him now. Scrabbling in his pocket as he ran, he found a five dollar note. This was no time to hesitate. Turning round he held up the note so the guard could see what it was. Then he dropped it. In the seconds it took the guard to stop and pick it up, Sonam was under the bridge and up onto the road. He had arrived in Nepal.

Chapter Twelve

Tashi was getting better. The injections, the acupuncture and the change in diet over the last few days had rapidly restored some movement to his back legs. They were still not as powerful as they should have been but at least his legs would now support his body and it was obvious that they were mending fast. The cub's walk was still a little odd but the dragging of the back half of his body by the front was now a thing of the past. The whole family was happy just to see him walking more normally.

Will had devised a series of what he liked to call 'lynx aerobics'. Basically this involved lying on his bedroom floor and playing his music far more loudly than was usually allowed. Then he would give Tashi a workout, forcing him to use his back legs, flexing and pushing them in a way that made the cub exercise his muscles. As they got stronger, Will would hold Tashi's front paws and make him walk just on his back legs, or roll him on his back and encourage him to kick at his arm. All of this was done to the beat of the music with Will imitating his mum's workout DVD and shouting out, "Right, now left and right and move those back legs, one, two, three, four...."

Jill and Steve had passed his room one day when one of these sessions was in progress and had laughed out loud at the sight of a bemused Tashi being manipulated by a very earnest looking Will.

"Yea, move those legs now, two, three, four..." Steve had joined in but Will had scowled at him before getting up to close his bedroom door.

As the cub got better, they began to make more serious plans for his eventual release. Simply to drive to some remote area and let him out of the boot of the car would be to invite certain death. It was doubtful if the cub would last more than a few days. He had to be taught how to hunt and how to kill for himself. He was already showing an encouraging interest in catching birds in the garden although he had not, as far as they knew, been successful yet. The nearest he had got was one Sunday afternoon when a hoopoe, looking wildly exotic with its bright colouring and its crested head, had landed on the lawn. Tashi had got very close before Steve scared the bird away. It was too beautiful to be killed, even by Tashi, and for Steve hoopoes had always been auspicious.

Just when everything seemed to be getting so much better, Will woke up one morning to find his bed in the most disgusting state. Although Tashi had never been house-trained, he had a cat's natural instinct for being clean. Now something had gone wrong. The bed was dirty and unpleasant smelling and one look at Tashi was enough to make Will realise that the cub was ill again. Almost overnight his fur had lost some of its shine and his eyes some of their gleam.

At breakfast time, the cub was listless and the quarter chicken Will offered was ignored. Tashi lay curled up in one corner of the living room showing no inclination to play – or even move.

"He's sick," Steve said. "What's scary about this is how fast his condition can change. One minute he's running around happily, the next his back legs are paralysed. One day he has a bright shiny coat and is chasing birds around the garden, the next he's slumped in a corner looking like death."

"Do you think it's serious?" Will asked. "It's only diarrhoea."

"Diarrhoea kills," said Steve. "You should know that by now. It may be a bit of a joke back home but you're living in a country where it's a killer. Thousands of kids die every year. And maybe animals too. They become dehydrated and it does permanent damage to their kidneys. We have to take it seriously."

"What do we do?"

"We get the faeces tested and see what's causing it. I'll get in touch with the zoo."

The test results were ready later that day. The cub's sickness was caused by some sort of parasite. If he was not treated quickly, he would die.

The zoo vet had again provided them with the medicine but he had warned them that it might not work. It was not, after all, meant for lynxes but for cattle. But they had to try. Tashi was looking worse and worse as every hour passed.

When Mike arrived at the spot where he had arranged to meet Sonam, he stopped the jeep and waited. There was no sign of the boy. He looked at his watch. It was already nine. If Sonam had made it across the border he should have been there hours ago. But there was no one in sight. For several minutes he hesitated.

Then slowly he came to believe that his little friend had been caught. He imagined Sonam in the back room of some bleak concrete building being interrogated by guards. In his head he could hear their shouted questions, their snarling contempt for this scruffy little Tibetan kid and he winced at the slaps and kicks that he could almost feel raining down on Sonam's recently healed but still vulnerable body. It wouldn't take them long to realise that he was harmless but their frustration at being posted to what many of them thought of as a foreign land sometimes came out in savage ways.

Disappointed but powerless, he got back into the jeep and told his driver to start the engine. It was only at that moment that he saw a figure lying by the roadside about a hundred metres ahead of him. He got out of the jeep and ran over to it. It was Sonam.

It took Mike only seconds to realise that the boy was in a bad way. He was covered in scratches and cuts from his flight through the forest, his clothes were ripped and he was soaking wet. The ground around him was damp. His hair was hanging limply and there was grit ground into his skin. He had a nasty cut on his leg to which his wet and blood-stained trousers were sticking. But more worrying than all of this was the raging temperature that Mike could feel from his forehead. Obviously Sonam's fever had returned. His exertions had been too much for his body to bear.

Mike shook him gently but Sonam did not stir. He felt his pulse. There was no doubt about it now, the boy was seriously ill. Mike picked him up and carried him to the jeep; his first job was to get him out of his wet clothes. Fortunately, he had spares of his own and it was not long before Sonam was dry, even if he did look a little ridiculous lying out on the back seat wearing clothes twice the size that he was.

Normally the journey from the Tibetan border to Kathmandu is one tourists like to linger over. The road winds through narrow valleys, following the rivers, or goes along the sides of steep hillsides with the Himalayas visible in the distance. But today Mike saw nothing. Urging his driver to go as fast as he safely could, he spent much of the ride twisted round uncomfortably in his seat to make sure that the barely conscious Sonam did not slip off the back seat and come to any further harm. At the same time, he was trying to sort out what he should do next.

It made no sense for Sonam to stay with him. He was out working for most of the day and Sonam needed more care than he could possibly give him. Besides, he was going to be away for the best part of the following week. With luck, Sonam would soon get better but at the moment he needed constant nursing.

They stopped only twice on the journey back to Kathmandu. Sonam was conscious enough on one of these occasions to be given something cold to drink and some aspirin to swallow. His surface injuries did not worry Mike at all but the fever did. The boy was looking flushed and he was again calling out in his sleep although Mike did not understand what he was saying. At least over the three hours of the journey his condition had not got any worse.

By now Mike had decided what to do. His writings and his studies had given him many contacts in the extensive Tibetan community in Kathmandu. He was particularly close to one of the lamas at Kopan Monastery in Boudhanath, one of the two major Tibetan centres in the city. He would take him there. The monks were skilled in medicine and Sonam would be well looked after. They would make sure that he was watched and prayed over night and day if necessary. And Mike would be able to visit him whenever he could.

As they neared Kathmandu, Mike told his driver to make for Boudhanath and it was not long before they reached the gates of Kopan.

Mike lifted Sonam carefully out of the car and stood for a moment in the great courtyard of the monastery. He walked up the steps to the assembly hall. The monks were praying inside and Mike could hear the strange unearthly sound of the chanting of the scriptures. He slipped off his shoes and crossed the threshold. The monks were seated in two lines that ran either side of the aisle which led to the great image of the Buddha. They looked up as Mike entered but there was no interruption to the chanting.

Instead of walking down the central aisle he turned right and walked around the back of the monks until he stood in front of the image of Avalokitesvara with his eleven heads and many arms.

"You see, Sonam, I place you before the image of the Bodhisattva of Compassion, the being that refused to become a Buddha until all of mankind is enlightened. There can be no greater love than that." He then sat cross-legged in front of the image and gazed at its golden surface as the light from the butter lamps flickered over it. Sonam slowly opened his eyes and saw the flickering of the gold and the flame. Sighing softly and smiling to himself, he closed his eyes again. He had seen the monk in maroon who now stood quietly behind Mike, waiting for him to turn and speak to him.

"Lama Pasang." Mike stood up and shook his hand warmly. "I have brought you a sick boy. I cannot look after him myself. Can you take good care of him?"

"Of course, Mike. Who is he?"

Briefly, Mike explained. When he had finished, the lama looked thoughtful. He stared at Sonam's face intently for several seconds.

"It's strange; he does not look like a nomad's son. Still, we will nurse him as best we can." He felt the boy's head and then he placed his hand over his heart. "I do not think there is much to worry about. With food, rest and care, he will be fine."

When Mike left, the lama had Sonam in his arms and was walking slowly up the staircase that led to the rooms where the monks cared for the sick. He entered one and lay the boy gently on the bed. Then he sat down and watched him as he slept. He ran his beads through his fingers and prayed that health would be restored to him.

When Sonam woke up several hours later, he was confused about where he was for the second time in a week. He pulled aside the rough blankets that covered him and found that he had been thoroughly washed. His wounds had been cleaned and some of them were now covered. There was no-one in the room. He got up and opened the door.

"Mike! Mike!" he shouted down the corridor. There was no reply. He shut the door and looked around his room. There was a painting of the Future Buddha on the wall. He studied it carefully for a moment and then went over to the window and looked out. The courtyard in front of him was painted white, with grass and flowers growing along the side of its paths. Slowly he looked up. Against the clear blue sky the roofs burned gold in the evening sun. Although he knew with certainty that he had never been there before, it all seemed strangely familiar.

With a smile he went back to his bed and fell deeply asleep within minutes.

Chapter Thirteen

Will was getting desperate. The medicine from the zoo vet had had no effect at all on Tashi and he was looking weaker and weaker. His fur was dull and lifeless and seemed to have changed from a smooth shine to dull clumps of dry hair. At one point he had struggled to his feet only to collapse again suddenly and for a moment Will had feared that the paralysis had returned. It hadn't but the cub's complete lack of energy and generally bedraggled condition was somehow even more alarming. Everyone in the household knew that Tashi was literally fighting for his life.

Steve had again emailed London Zoo, sending details of the analysis. This time they had waited impatiently for Simon Goodfield's reply. When it came it was not encouraging.

Hi Steve,
Thanks for your mail. I'm glad to hear that the paralysis has gone and that the cub is moving around more freely. As for the diarrhoea, there is, as you can imagine, nothing made for the treatment of lynxes! The only thing I can suggest is that you give him the drug that we use in the treatment of hookworm in

cattle and pigs. Be warned – it is expensive. There is also some risk – in rare cases it can be fatal. It will almost certainly be unavailable in Nepal but I can get some on the next flight to Nepal from London if you want it.
Let me know.
Kind regards,
Simon

Steve had wasted no time sending back a reply and they had received a further mail a couple of hours later.

Hi again Steve,
The drug is being couriered out on the Qatar flight tomorrow. You need to meet it.
You will need to weigh the cub to make sure that you give it the correct dosage, which is by body weight. Don't overdo it – he's pretty small compared to a cow or a pig! Administer 0.2 micrograms per kilo. Don't be concerned if the cub starts to twitch and behave oddly for a few hours. This is normal but it can be pretty alarming! It's a neurological side-effect but it's usually harmless.
Good luck!
Simon

The Qatar flight from London was due to land in forty-eight hours. Steve and Jill both doubted that the cub would last that long. They had tried feeding him but he would only take food that was more or less forced down his throat. The last time they had tried he had choked. After that, they had simply tried to get him to drink water. But even that was difficult and it was obvious he was losing far more fluids than they were able to replace. There was a gloomy silence as they sat over the remains of breakfast. Finally, Will broke it.

"Dad, there has to be something we can do. There has to be."

"What?" asked Steve. "We have to be patient and wait for the flight. The local stuff didn't work and I'm not prepared to risk it again. These drugs are pretty tough on a healthy body, let alone one that is suffering as much as that one seems to be."

"But if we don't do something he's going to die." The cub had spent breakfast time lying on Will's lap, his eyes closed and the tip of his tongue sticking out between his front teeth. He had hardly moved at all. "He's going to die." And suddenly tears were rolling down Will's cheeks in a stream he couldn't stop.

"Come on, Will, he's not dead yet. Don't give up hope. Look, let's take him and get him blessed. It's a miracle he's survived so far, let's ask for another one." Jill looked into the boy's doubting eyes. "There's nothing to lose, Will."

Will nodded. His parents were regular visitors to the monasteries, as were a number of his parents' friends, even those who were not devout Buddhists. They were peaceful places to escape from daily routine, quiet and out of the way. Will liked their calm and their colours, the oranges and reds of the painting and the giant sized statues of Buddha that were quite frightening when you first saw them but then oddly comforting when you knew they were there.

He gathered Tashi from his lap and stood up. "Alright, if we are going, let's go."

Boudhanath was only a few minutes away if you drove quickly but that was out of the question in Kathmandu. The streets were full of people walking in every direction and ignoring the cars. Bicycles were everywhere and little motorbikes overtook the car both on the inside and the outside, often at the same time. They threaded their way through the chaos, swerving dangerously around the cows that ambled towards them without a care in the world. Whatever his mood, Will never failed to enjoy these car rides because you never knew what you would see next. But today he was just irritated and impatient.

"Get out of the way," he shouted out of the window at a massive white bull sitting in the middle of the road but he was wasting his breath and Jill turned around to tell him off.

"Stop it, Will. Don't be so impatient."

"Well..." and he sat muttering to himself for the rest of the journey.

They left the car at the main gates. The focus of the many monasteries in the area was a stupa, a massive, solid dome, painted white and covered in prayer flags. It had been a holy site for hundreds and hundreds of years and was still a centre of pilgrimage, not only for Buddhists in Nepal but also for pilgrims from Tibet and other Himalayan countries. At any time of day there were dozens, even hundreds, of pilgrims walking clockwise, turning prayer wheels and mumbling prayers. Its highest point was a series of thirteen circles of gold and from the very top of this glittering spire great strings of coloured prayer flags stretched out in all directions. Against a deep blue sky it was an unforgettable sight and one to which even locals returned endlessly.

But today the beauty of the stupa was lost on Will. Normally he enjoyed looking in the circle of shops that surrounded it and spotting the Tibetan people who had travelled, often for weeks, to visit it. Now he was interested only in getting to the monastery. Brushing aside the keen traders and the pushy beggars, he hurried through the crowds with his parents almost running to keep up with him.

He paused only when he got to the bottom of the steps that led up to the great doors of Kopan Monastery. Holding Tashi tight to his chest he began to climb the steps. He took off his shoes at the door and stepped through. It was silent inside and hundreds of butter lamps burned with still flames. His eyes adjusted slowly to the half-darkness and then he made his way down the centre aisle to stand before the image of the Buddha. He felt very small beside it.

Steve and Jill stood quietly in the background and prayed for a few moments before speaking to one of the monks. They told him about the dying cub and explained that they had brought it to be blessed. The monk said he would find someone and left.

Some minutes later he returned and asked them to follow him. He led them away from the main part of the monastery and across a courtyard to a chapel rarely visited by outsiders. There they found a lama. He did not look up when they entered but he gestured to them to sit down and wait until he had finished quietly chanting his text.

Will sat still, holding the cub against his chest. Tashi had barely moved since they had left the house except to nuzzle ever closer. Now he had his head under Will's shirt, resting against the boy's bare skin.

The lama finished his text and stood up. He smiled in greeting and then went over to Will to take hold of the lynx cub. He stroked its head and ran his fingers the length of its back. He pulled back Tashi's eyelids and breathed into his nose. Finally, he placed the cub on the low table in front of him and started to pray. He chanted for a long time, occasionally stroking the cub. Although Will did not understand what was being said, he began to recognise the rhythms and the repetitions of the chanting. When he had finished, the lama turned to Will and his parents.

"I have prayed over him and blessed him. Perhaps it will do some good, if not in this life then in the next. Tell me, how do you come to have such an unusual pet? I have seen them many times in the high Himalayas in Tibet but never in Kathmandu."

"He was brought to us by some friends from Tibet," said Steve. "They bought him on the street in Shigatse. Apparently he was just about to be sold to a Chinese trader. I guess if he had been he would have been made into a potion by now."

The monk smiled. "Unfortunately that is what happens to many of these beautiful creatures. It is the bones that are supposed to be of great medicinal value. Most valuable of all, of course, is the tiger itself. Then the snow leopard, then the lynx." He picked up the cub and straightened out its back leg. He traced the upper part of it with his finger. "You see how long the bone is? That is why it is prized. There is even a wine made from tiger bones. What is the cub's name?"

"Tashi," said Will.

"Ah, a name that means 'good fortune', so let us hope for him that he is well named."

He paused for a moment and returned the cub to Will. "I'm afraid your little friend does look very sick. Have you given him medicine?"

Steve told him about the drugs that were due to arrive on the next flight. "Do you think he will last until then?"

The lama smiled. "Who can tell? If his time has come, he will pass to his next life. You should pray for him yourselves. I will teach you a mantra, a prayer, to speak over him. It is a mantra of the Future Buddha."

For the next ten minutes they struggled with the strange sounding Tibetan words until the monk was satisfied that they could pronounce them properly. Then he stood up. "One more thing I can do for you. I will write out this mantra and then it can be hung around his neck. Can you wait a few moments?" He bowed slightly to them and left.

"Well, do you think it did any good?" asked Will. He found it difficult to keep the impatience out of his voice. "He doesn't look any better yet."

"Don't be silly, Will, you'll have to give it time. Maybe he'll get better, maybe he won't. But he will die a better death for being blessed."

"I don't care about his next life – if he has one. I want him to get better now so he can enjoy this one. Anyway, I don't know that I believe in all this reincarnation stuff."

The door opened again and the lama reappeared. In his hand he held a small silver box and a scroll of paper. He showed them the mantra he had written, then rolled it up tightly and put it inside the box. He threaded a string through the loops at the edge of the box and gave it to Will. "There you are. When he is quiet you can put it around his neck – but be careful not to choke him. Perhaps it would be better if you were to hang it on the wall just over the place he sleeps. It will do him good."

Will slipped the string over his own head and nestled the cub back against his chest. The mantra sat comfortably against the cub's head. The lama smiled when he saw it. "Just one thing. I have a friend who is very anxious to see your cub. You see, he once had one of his own."

He looked past Will and his parents to the small doorway behind them. Standing there very quietly, but watching them intently, was a boy of about Will's age. It was Sonam.

Chapter Fourteen

In the days that followed, Sonam and Will often talked about that first meeting. Sonam had not doubted from the moment he had seen the cub that it was the same one that he had rescued but he had no desire to claim him back. Besides, he knew Tashi was no longer his. He had been sold. Money had changed hands.

The telling of the cub's story had taken some time and three languages. The lama had helped at first, translating from Tibetan to English. Then Will had realised that Sonam spoke a little Nepali, so they had left the adults to talk to each other while they tried to hold a conversation with a lot of gestures and not much vocabulary. This had rapidly reduced both of them to laughter and it was not long before they were behaving like old friends. When it was time for Will and his parents to go, Sonam had begged the lama to let him go with them.

At first he had looked doubtful. "You are still not strong, Sonam. You need rest. You have much to learn and I have much to teach you. But go with them. Stay until the medicine from England arrives and see if the cub can be cured. Then come back to me and be prepared to study hard."

And that was what had happened. Sonam had spent the night in the spare bed in Will's room and they had waited impatiently the whole of the next day for the drugs to be brought from the airport by Steve's driver. There had been little change in Tashi's condition all this time. He moved as little as possible and though they all tried hard, no one could get him to eat anything. All they could do was make sure that he drank water, mixed with salt and sugar, to replace the lost body fluids and even that had to be more or less squirted down his throat while he wriggled and squirmed away from it.

Finally the capsule arrived. But when it was time for the actual injection, a sudden nervousness came over the family.

"If this doesn't work," said Steve, "we are in trouble. This is our last hope." He opened the box and looked at the tiny glass container of clear liquid and the small syringe that lay beside it. Everything depended on this.

"What about the twitching?" Will asked.

Steve had been reading the accompanying leaflet, hardly any of which made sense to him.

"That's a risk we have to take."

"Don't worry too much about the side-effects, Will," said his mother. "It's the main effect we have to worry about. Let's face it: if this doesn't cure Tashi, it looks very much as though he's going to die." She said it kindly and put her arm around his shoulders. It was always difficult, the balance between honesty and comfort but she felt strongly that they all had to face up to the possibility that the cub might die. And if it didn't, well, they were hoping to release it into the wild and so the cub would be gone in a different way.

Looking at Tashi, it was becoming increasingly difficult to believe that he could survive. His fur had lost all of its gloss and was faded and mangy. His eyes were dull and remained shut most of the time. He barely moved and they had managed to feed him water only by inserting the end of Will's water pistol gently into his mouth. "Just skin and bone," Will had heard his father tell Chuck on the phone and that had just about summed it up.

"Well, here we go." Steve was holding the capsule in the air and drawing the fluid down into the syringe. They had weighed the cub and worked out the correct dosage, although they had talked for some time about whether body weight meant the weight now or the weight when the cub had been well. To be safe, they decided on the present weight.

"Stop!" said Sonam, holding up his hand. "Wait!"

Steve paused with the needle against the fur. Sonam rushed off to Will's bedroom and came back seconds later with the silver box containing the mantra. He placed it against the cub's head and started to chant quietly, nodding to Steve that he should carry on. Tashi barely moved as the needle slid in and in a few moments it was done. All they could do now was wait.

For some time nothing happened. Then the cub started to twitch and shake. Although they had been prepared for this, the reality was much worse than they had anticipated. Tashi was suddenly transformed into a puppet whose limbs were being jerked by savagely pulled strings. It was almost too much for Will to bear.

"We shouldn't have done it," he screamed, "we shouldn't have done it. We've gone and killed him!"

It took his mother some time to calm him but finally she and Steve between them persuaded him and Sonam to get out of the house for the next couple of hours and let the medicine do its work. They could do nothing; they would only be distressed; it was better they were out. And besides, Sonam had seen nothing of Kathmandu yet. Reluctantly, Will and Sonam took to the streets.

It was not very far from their house to the centre of town and so they decided to walk. For Sonam, everything was a surprise. After the muddied streets of Shigatse, the biggest town he had been to, Kathmandu was noisy and fast and full of life. Sometimes their language and their mime ran out, as when Will tried to explain that DVD shops rented out DVDs, but the boys had by this time formed such a close bond that what couldn't be said seemed not to matter. Sonam was amazed at the wide variety of goods on sale and Will took great delight in introducing him to chocolate bars and, a little later, ice cream.

By the time they reached the centre, Sonam was choking on the petrol fumes and beginning to find the constant noise painful to his ears. He had felt very sad at one point on their walk when they had passed one of the little butcher's sheds. The sight of the tied-up, miserable-looking goats outside it had been bad enough but the blood and the skinned carcasses on the floor inside the shed had brought back memories of his father and mother and of the day they had slaughtered their own sheep. In the first few days after he ran away he had thought little about his family – he had been too ill – but as he had started to recover in the monastery his thoughts had returned to them again and again. One day, he knew, he would go back. But not yet. And as they admired the Royal Palace and the gilded roofs of the temples and the dozens of little shrines that appeared to be on every street corner, his sadness vanished and he was overtaken by the excitement of being in a strange and bustling place.

They were now in the tourist area of Kathmandu, a collection of small streets lined with cheap hotels and restaurants. The streets were busy but instead of local people doing their shopping and going about their daily business, there were tourists from all over the world, drawn to Kathmandu by its exotic sounding name, its culture and Nepal's mountain trekking. Sonam had never before seen so many different nationalities and asked Will endless questions about who these people were and where they came from and how much it had cost them. He was also surprised to see in some shop windows turquoise and coral and silver necklaces like the ones his mother wore. Looking harder, he could also see old pots and trunks like the ones he had seen in other people's tents and houses in Tibet. He did not understand what they were doing there.

To Will all of this seemed familiar but, although he answered Sonam's questions cheerfully enough, there was nothing sufficiently different about it to hold his attention and stop him from thinking about Tashi. The hooting cars and the street vendors who constantly tried to sell him flutes and knives that he did not want were beginning to annoy him in a way they rarely did. A small boy who offered him Tiger Balm was almost physically pushed aside. Will remembered just in time that the only thing that the medicine had in common with the animal was its name.

Sonam was walking just ahead of Will when he stopped and began peering into a particular shop window. It was much like many others, full of carved sandalwood boxes and beautifully painted papier-mâché animals. But Sonam was staring past these into the interior. Will joined him and slowly realised what he had been staring at. On a rack at the back of the shop was a row of jackets made out of the skins of wild animals.

Before Sonam could say anything, Will had leapt up the steps into the shop and pushed aside the only customer. He turned on the shopkeeper.

"What are these? What are these doing here?"

"These animal skins, sir, made into coats. Some very rare. This one, for example, is a snow leopard. Very beautiful, very rare."

"But the snow leopard is protected. Hardly anyone ever sees it." Will was getting angrier by the minute.

"That is correct sir." The shopkeeper was eager to please and knew from experience that these Western kids had wealthy parents that could lead to a future sale. "But as you see we can provide the skins. We have our friends in the mountains who can bring these things to us." He smiled unpleasantly.

"You mean poachers, that's what you mean." Will's anger had turned to sudden fury and he found himself shouting. "That's illegal. It's illegal to sell these things. The police should arrest you."

The shopkeeper's smile had vanished and he too was beginning to get angry. "Really, this is none of your business. Kindly leave my shop. Go, get out of my shop."

But with a cry of rage Will grabbed the rack of furs and pulled it to the ground. He tore the jackets off their hangers and then hurled them around the shop. The shopkeeper was too surprised to do anything but when he saw what was happening he tried to grab Will and pin him down. Sonam, who until then had watched in amazement, jumped forward to help Will. The shopkeeper quickly realised he couldn't handle two mad boys on his own and rushed off to get help.

"Will, what are you doing? Animals dead already. You gone mad? Police, police will come."

"I don't care. Let them come." Will was blazing with anger. "The police should be arresting him, not me. It's illegal to sell these skins, don't you understand that? Illegal. There are international agreements and things."

This was all a bit beyond Sonam who knew all too well that if they did not get away in a hurry the police would come for them. And while they would hesitate to be rough with a Westerner, he would have no such protection. He looked around the shop. There were coats everywhere and the shelves had been cleared of their goods, which now lay in jumbled heaps on the floor. He might have succeeded in getting his friend away if at that moment Will had not discovered one particular jacket hidden under a pile of others. There was no mistaking the colour or the markings. It was lynx.

When the police arrived a few minutes later with the owner, they found a shop in chaos and a young boy sitting in the middle of the floor crying hysterically. In his hands he held the lynx jacket. He still had sufficient anger left to turn on the shopkeeper.

"You... How dare you? How can you sell these coats? How can you have the blood of so many creatures on your hands?"

The shopkeeper ignored him. "Give me that. That coat is worth hundreds of dollars. Give it to me. You will pay for the damage you have done."

"Hundreds of dollars?" The question was Sonam's.

"Yes, hundreds." And Sonam remembered how hard his father had struggled to get a handful of dollars for the skin and bones in Shigatse. It was only then that he realised how much they had been cheated.

"You must do something to them," the shopkeeper screamed angrily. "You call yourselves policemen and yet you let young hooligans destroy my shop under your very noses."

The police were actually watching all this with some amusement. Had Sonam been on his own, they would almost certainly have taken him to their police post and given him a thorough beating to discourage him from causing trouble again. But Will's presence made them cautious. Besides, the shopkeeper was rich and rude so they did not feel any great desire to protect him. They would probably have let the boys go with a warning if the shopkeeper had not made so much fuss.

After a lot of shouting, during which quite a large crowd gathered outside, Will phoned his father. The police guarded the entrance to the shop, keeping the boys inside, until Steve arrived. He was not pleased.

"What on earth have you been doing Will? I don't care how strongly you feel about this, this is no way to behave."

He ignored Will's indignant attempts to justify himself and paid the shopkeeper some compensation. There had not been a lot of actual damage and it soon became obvious that the large sums he had demanded were simply an attempt to make money out of the incident. But he was still furious when they left.

Once they got into the car, Will felt the full force of his father's anger. He struggled to tell Steve about the skins and the coats but his father wasn't prepared to listen; under no circumstances was his son going to cause a scene like that. Nor did he have any right to damage other people's property. Did he understand?

His mother was a little more understanding but no more sympathetic. Will was soon on his way to bed with no supper and Sonam on his way back to the monastery. But not even the angry parents could send the boys off without telling them that Tashi was already looking a great deal better.

Chapter Fifteen

Over the next few weeks it became obvious that Tashi was finally recovering. The change was dramatic. His eyes were brighter and his fur glossier and he quickly regained the sense of fun and mischief that he had shown as a young cub. He was also growing fast. With the parasites out of his system and a proper diet established, he seemed to get bigger and stronger every time they looked at him. And so it was inevitable that the family began to talk about releasing him into the wild.

"Sooner or later, Will, he has to go. We don't know how long we shall be living here and I can't imagine anyone else would be very keen to take on a fully grown lynx." Jill was trying to get Will used to the idea.

"He could go to the zoo. They'd be nice to him there."

"Would you really like to think of Tashi stuck in some cage that was too small for him, being stared at by hundreds of visitors every day? Do you really think he'd like that?"

"He might."

"Now you're just being silly, Will. He would hate it and you would hate the idea of it, you know you would."

She was right of course. Will hated the idea of Tashi stuck behind bars. He really liked the zoo vet and recognised that he loved and cared for the animals but he would only see Tashi if and when he was ill. Otherwise Tashi would just be pointed and gawped at by streams of people who had nothing better to do. Nonetheless, he found the idea of letting him go a hard one to accept.

"Somebody might want him. Have you asked everybody?" He emphasised the last word. "And besides, we might not leave for a long time. We might never leave."

"We will some time," said Jill. And that had more or less ended the conversation.

Will had not seen Sonam for some time since the incident with the shopkeeper and he was feeling rather guilty about the whole thing. It had been his fault from beginning to end and he was worried that Sonam might have been in serious trouble with the lama when he got back to the monastery. There was no question that he would have found out even if Sonam had kept quiet. Kathmandu was a city of rumours and nearly all of them, however strange, turned out to be true.

In fact, he need not have worried. Sonam was spending his days happily. He had been true to his word and had been studying hard. His days had a calm sense of routine about them and because of his recent illness he was not required to get up during the night or in the early morning to pray with the others. His long nights of sleep had healed him, together with a good diet and the medicines provided by the monks. He was feeling strong and healthy. He was also a good pupil, so good that the lama had found it increasingly difficult to believe that Sonam's background was what he said it was. And yet the boy was so honest in everything he did and said that he could not possibly be lying.

As the lama went through the teachings of the sacred texts, Sonam showed a quick understanding and a keen mind. The Buddhist teaching tradition encourages dispute and it was not long before teacher and pupil were engaged in fierce debate. But always the arguments were calm and courteous, with Sonam quickly acknowledging the superior learning and understanding of his guide. It did not take the lama long to realise that Sonam was the most outstanding pupil he had ever had.

He also realised that the boy would not stay long at the monastery. They had spent many hours talking about his family and life in Tibet and as time passed Sonam would refer to it with increasing frequency. It was becoming obvious that he would return before too long. But although he would miss his pupil, this did not trouble the lama. He knew that their lessons were only the beginning of Sonam's learning.

When the monk arrived at the lama's teaching room to say that there was an urgent phone call for Sonam, he was in the middle of studying a particularly difficult text. He knew at once that it would be Will. He looked up anxiously at the lama, who nodded. Sonam left the room as quietly as he could and then tore down the stairs to take the landline phone.

"Sonam? Sonam? Is that you? It's Will here. Sonam, you have to help me. Something terrible has happened."

Sonam struggled to understand Will's Nepali but the panic in his voice was enough to convince him that something was seriously wrong. "What is it, Will?"

"It's Tashi. He's escaped. He was in the garden but now he's gone. Please Sonam, you've got to help me look for him."

"Coming. Now."

Sonam ran back up the stairs to explain what was happening and to get permission to leave. Within minutes he was clutching a tattered twenty rupee note and getting into one of the tuk-tuks that buzzed around the roads near Boudhanath. It took him no time to get to Will's house, although it felt forever. When he got there it looked empty.

Sonam went inside and stood in the hall.

"Will, Will, are you here?" There was no reply. He made his way to Will's bedroom, calling out as he went, and opened the door. Will was lying on his bed staring at the ceiling. He didn't even turn his head when Sonam walked in.

"What has happened Will?" Sonam could see the grey marks of tears streaked down Will's face. "Why are you not looking for Tashi?"

"It's no good, Sonam, he could be anywhere. I've been all around the neighbourhood. I didn't see a sign of him. I couldn't ask people if they had seen a lynx, it would have caused chaos. The only thing is to hope that he comes back when he's hungry."

"No, Will, we have to look for him. He might do damage... kill chickens... eat them. People will hit him with stones. Or shoot him. Lying here is no good. Get up. We must find him. I'll help you. Come on." By this time Sonam was pulling Will off the bed and onto the floor.

"I've already looked; it's hopeless."

"Will, what is the matter? Do you care about Tashi or not? Do you want to get him back or not?"

"Of course I do."

"Then stop feeling sorry for yourself. I'm going to look. Get up and come with me."

Sonam was only a few steps out of the room when he heard Will behind him. Together they started to look around the garden. As he searched for prints and clues, Sonam suddenly imagined he was back by the stream in Tibet. For a moment he longed to be there. Soon... But his full attention returned sharply when he found what he was looking for.

"Look. Prints."

"The garden is full of prints..." Will started to reply dismissively but Sonam had already moved on, putting together the clues to Tashi's escape. It looked as though he had been lying on the grass when he had suddenly got up to chase something. Whatever it was, it had moved quickly because in only a couple of strides Tashi appeared to have reached full stretch. The last set of prints in the garden was just before the perimeter wall and they were deep, suggesting that Tashi had jumped at that point. At least they knew now in which direction he had started off.

Will looked at the six feet high wall in surprise. Sonam caught the look. "This is nothing," he said. "You should see one when it's really moving. Let's go."

They climbed the wall and Sonam picked out the print in the earth on the other side. Will could hardly see what they were following until Sonam pointed out to him the broken twigs or the flattened grass stalks or the half-print in the mud. He had to admit that Sonam was pretty good at it. Once they nearly caught up with the cub in a narrow alley way.

Tashi was standing at the end and turned to look at them, even moving a few steps towards them at the sound of Will's voice. But when Will had moved forward with the intention of grabbing his collar, he had suddenly bounded over the wall, pausing only to glance over his shoulder as if to say, "This is fun, follow me if you can!"

And of course they did, across gardens and down narrow tracks and across the occasional road. Even in this part of Kathmandu, so close to the centre, there were fields and trees and footpaths between houses rather than roads.

They had been chasing Tashi for perhaps twenty minutes when they came across a small group of children standing wide-eyed in the doorway of a house. They were watching a snarling mongrel that kept running half way across a building plot and then, tucking its tail between its legs, running back again. They were giggling with excitement and pushing each other off the step on which they were perched. At first Sonam and Will could not see what they were staring at. Then one of the little girls pointed across the rubble to where Tashi was crouching in the shade of an old brick wall, ears laid back along his head, eyes fixed intently on his prey.

With horror Will realised that his target was a young goat. He jumped forward to stop Tashi but Sonam grabbed him.

"Let him, Will. Let's see if he can kill it."

"Sonam you idiot, I can't. That's somebody's goat. It's not a wild animal. It belongs to somebody." Will didn't know whether to laugh or not. In the end he did. "Oh well, we can always pay. It's male, so it will get killed anyway. Whether it gets killed now or later, it makes no difference. And we'll get to see if Tashi can handle his own food."

Sonam turned to the children and told them to be quiet. They had been getting increasingly noisy as the lynx crept nearer to the kid. Suddenly frightened, they were immediately silent. Even the dog stopped barking.

Will and Sonam watched as Tashi slowly closed the gap between the kid and himself. He was moving so slowly that he hardly seemed to be moving at all but the ground was covered in a surprisingly short time. The goat seemed completely unaware of the danger it was in. When Tashi was within springing distance, he settled himself into the ground before accelerating into a leap that brought the kid crashing down. It was dead in seconds.

One of the little boys started screaming and soon the rest were shouting. Sonam tried again to quieten them but this time he had no success. One of the girls ran off to tell the goat's owner. As she ran she shouted, "Chituwa! Chituwa! Leopard! Leopard!"

"That's done it," Will groaned. "There'll be a mob here any minute. Come on Sonam, we have to get Tashi out of here or they'll try to kill him."

But the boys didn't move, watching fascinated instead as Tashi stood over the carcass of his kill, sniffing at it curiously. Then he began to eat. Seeing the meat, the dog bounded forward but scampered back in terror as Tashi growled from deep in his throat. He would protect his kill.

One of the other children was crying and Will thought for a horrible moment it might have been her kid. But it wasn't. She did, however, know who the owner was, "big man", and Will prepared himself for the row that would break out when he learned what had happened. Well, that was in the future. The immediate problem was to recapture Tashi.

That proved easier than they had expected. Tashi growled as they approached the kill but there was no way he was either going to leave the goat or attack Will, so slipping the chain over his neck and fastening it securely proved no particular problem. By now a small crowd was gathering and they could hear in the distance the sound of the little girl's voice and the answering shouts of the men in the fields. Will started to half haul, half carry Tashi back home while Sonam carried the remains of the kid, keeping it as close to Tashi's nose as he could. Will asked the name of the goat's owner and promised the children that they would return that evening and settle their debt. But they had not gone twenty metres before they met a mob of angry men coming towards them.

"For heaven's sake help me explain, Sonam. If you don't, we are done for and so is Tashi."

There was no denying what had happened. With the dead kid and the lynx as evidence, the story told itself. The men were shouting loudly and the owner of the kid was demanding an absurd figure as compensation. They were armed with sticks and the hoes they had been using in the fields. At one point Will was convinced that they were about to be attacked. He promised the owner full compensation if he would only let him go and get the money. At first he wouldn't listen and Will thought they were going to be locked in one of the houses until the money was brought. Finally, Sonam, who had remained remarkably calm throughout all this, persuaded the men to follow them to Will's house where they would get their money. They were still muttering angrily and one of them was demanding that Tashi be released so that they could kill him but the truth was that the men were scared to touch Will and wary of what Tashi might do if he were released from his chain.

Will's parents had already returned and they listened by turns fascinated and horrified to the story the boys had to tell. The mob had quietened down considerably by the time they had reached the house and only the owner of the kid and two of his friends had been allowed into the compound while the others stayed restlessly outside the gates. After a lot of haggling, a price had been agreed. Steve had paid willingly to get rid of the men even though the figure was double the goat's real value.

When they were free to talk it all over, they had to admit that it had its funny side too. None of them could disguise their delight that Tashi had proved beyond all possible doubt that he could kill for himself.

"Well, that's it, I guess," said Steve. "He's proved he can do it. He may find it more difficult in the wild but there's not a lot we can do about that."

"What are we going to do about him escaping?" Jill asked.

Will laughed. "You should have seen him this afternoon. He went over walls as if they weren't there. It'll be pretty hard to keep him in unless we build a giant cage."

"Not necessary, I think," said Sonam quietly and there was silence for a moment as they realised what he meant.

It was time for Tashi to go.

Chapter Sixteen

Once the decision to release Tashi had been made, and the following Saturday agreed as the day, Will's family put all their energy into preparing for it. News of the lynx's escape and the killing of the goat had spread rapidly through the neighbourhood and there was a sudden growth of interest in Tashi as well as an understandable fear that he might escape again. Steve and Jill spent some time reassuring their worried neighbours that the cub was completely under control and that in any case it would only be with them for a few more days.

Steve and the boys had spent hours in the garden putting up two strong pole structures and running a steel rope between them. It ran almost the entire length of the garden, stopping six feet short of both boundary walls to avoid any possibility of Tashi being able to climb them. His chain was attached to the wire with a steel clip like the ones mountaineers use so Tashi could run the length of the wire in perfect safety but with no chance of escape. When he wasn't in the garden he was loose in the house but always with two closed doors between him and the garden. They were taking no chances.

Tashi had continued to grow stronger and he looked healthy. His coat had a high gloss and his eyes were bright. He looked alert and was always hungry. With some misgivings they had started to feed him the chickens live, releasing them in the garden within stalking distance of the reach of his chain. He killed cleanly.

The evenings had been full of phone calls and farewells. Chuck had called from the States and was delighted that the cub was going to be released. After all the problems, he had expected Tashi to spend the rest of his life in a cage.

"You wouldn't recognise him now," Steve had said. "He really is a different animal. He's grown so much you wouldn't believe it. I'm sure he's going to be fine."

Sonam spent the days with Will and the evenings and early mornings studying at the monastery. He had been very anxious that Mike should be there when they released Tashi and was relieved when he had phoned. He had been out of town for a few days and was very excited when he heard how much better the cub was and that they thought it was ready to be freed into the wild. Of course he'd be there. It seemed that everything was finally coming together.

On Friday evening they took Tashi to the zoo vet for a final check-up. Mr Shrestha was as charming as ever and gave him a very thorough looking over. Finally he turned to Will.

"You have done a very good job. You know, when I first saw this cub, although he is not so much of a cub now, I thought there was no chance that he would even live. This may seem hard-hearted to you but over the years I have seen many different animals 'rescued' by foreigners. They think they are doing something wonderful but mostly the animals die. In many cases they would have been better off left where they were. Nature's way is often the kindest though it may not look that way at the time. But you have worked hard with Tashi and you deserve your success."

He put his arm around Will's shoulders before carrying on.

"Tomorrow you are going to do the hardest thing anyone can do. You are going to let go of something you love because you believe it will be better for him if you do. When you drive away from Tashi you will feel sick and your heart will hurt as if it will never stop. If that happens, try to think of something else. Try to think instead of this magnificent animal running and hunting in one of the great open spaces of the world, living close to his instincts and his own heart. See him for what he is, rather than what you would like him to be."

As he lay in bed that night, Will thought a lot about what the vet had said and he went to sleep imagining the lynx running wild in the forests and across the open high plateau.

In his bed at the monastery, Sonam was also dreaming of the lynx. He saw the animal's head close to his and the cat was staring into his eyes. Sonam stared back until he felt himself drawn into the pupils of the eyes and falling down through their space. But it was not a fall that produced panic. Instead he found himself floating, turning around and around like the seedpod of a tree until he came gently to rest on the ground. There he felt the warmth of the fire outside his mother's tent and, staring into the blackness of the night, he could just make out the gleam of two eyes moving away from him until they vanished into the surrounding darkness.

The lama was not surprised when Sonam came to him early the next morning and told him that he had decided to return home. The lynx was to be released on the Nepal-Tibet border. It was an obvious chance to get a lift part of the way.

"I had expected this. But tell me, little one, what will you do when you return? First you will search for your mother and father. But when you have found them and spent some time with them, what will you do then?"

Sonam shrugged. The lama laughed.

"Perhaps you are right. Who knows? But Sonam, you have learned a lot here. Do not forget the things you have learned. You have your own life to make and your own destiny to fulfil. Don't forget that."

The Landrover was already full by the time it arrived to collect Sonam. The lama had been asked to come as well, to bless the future life of the lynx and offer prayers for his protection. Steve and Jill were in the front while Will was sitting next to the crate in which Tashi lay. The cub was shivering slightly in response to the unfamiliar noise and smells of the Landrover. The lama sat next to Mike and Sonam squashed in beside Will.

For some time the boys said very little. Then Sonam spoke. "Will, I am not coming back with you today. When Tashi goes, I am going too. I am going back to my family."

Will was shocked. He had never really thought of Sonam having a family although he had talked about his parents from time to time. He had been very brave until then but the thought of losing both of his best friends at the same time was almost too much.

"Why, Sonam? Why now? You don't have to go, do you?"

"Yes, Will. I have to go. It is right. Right time." After that they talked of other things, in particular of the times they had spent together and they laughed as they agreed a score of one-all for getting each other into serious trouble.

"You got me into trouble in the shop; I got you into trouble with the goat. One-one. That's fair." Sonam grinned and the two boys laughed aloud at the memories.

"Those two are taking it well," said Steve, smiling at Jill as he changed down a gear to go around the next hairpin.

It was about four hours later that they finally arrived at the place where they intended to release the lynx. They had gone almost the whole way down the main road to the border and then taken a tiny dirt track turning off to the left. In wet weather it would have been almost impassable, even in a Landrover. But the day was sunny and dry and the Landrover was able to get well up into the hills before the forest closed in on them and the increasing narrowness of the track forced them to get out and walk. They unloaded the crate containing Tashi and the bags with the food and fruit juices they had brought for their picnic lunch. Will clipped Tashi onto his chain and led him along the tiny path that led up through the forest.

For some time they all struggled and sweated up the hill, except for Sonam who didn't seem to notice the steep gradient. Then suddenly the path dropped down swiftly into a narrow valley. It held a fast flowing stream and they finally stopped at one of the few points where the valley widened into a small clearing and the stream slowed down to form a series of pools and shallows. They had seen nobody for an hour.

"How on earth did you know about this place, Mike?" muttered Steve.

"Trade secret! No seriously, it's one of the places where Tibetan refugees have crossed into Nepal when the main border has been too heavily guarded. This stream runs straight out of Tibet. We are very close to the border; we might even be across it for all I know. Once you get into the hills like this there is nothing to mark the boundary. Have you got your passport?" He grinned.

Jill was organising the food. She and Steve had planned the release carefully. First they would all sit around together and eat; then the lama would pray over Tashi; then the lynx would be set free. They would watch Tashi until they could see him no more and then, immediately, they would leave and drive back home.

Mike was busy explaining to Sonam where he must go. "Compared to last time, this one is easy. Follow the stream. After half a kilometre or so, this stream will be joined by another that comes in from the right. Take that right fork and follow it. By then you will have crossed the border and be in Tibet. Continue upstream until you see a ruined herder's hut. There is a track that leads to it and past it. Follow that track for about an hour and you will come to the main Shigatse road. Then start looking for rides. And don't forget to say hello to Tsering for me when you go past!"

It sounded easy – and this time Sonam was fit.

Considering the occasion, the meal was a happy one. No-one wanted a miserable parting and whenever Will was tempted to feel sorry for himself the vet's words came back to him. Even looking at Tashi was exciting. He was more alert than Will had ever seen him, his nose constantly wrinkling and twitching as he pulled scents out of the air, his eyes following the butterflies and the slightest movements of the humans.

Too soon the meal was finished and the boxes repacked. The lama stood up and went over to Tashi. He rested his hand on his head and quietly recited the mantra of the Future Buddha. For several seconds the lynx stood absolutely still as the words flowed over him. The lama finished his chant, took the silver amulet box containing the mantra and touched it to Tashi's head. The time for his release had come.

Steve unclipped Tashi, picked him up and held him for a second, and then passed him to Jill who did the same. Then she handed him to Will. "You take him, Will, you and Sonam. Go on," she said as he hesitated, "we have talked about this. You and Sonam take him. You two must set him free."

Will took the lynx in his arms and began to walk upstream. Sonam was still talking to Mike and to the lama but he soon caught up.

"*Bistare*, Will, slowly. Be gentle. You'll squash him!" Sonam smiled. And it was true. Will was hugging the animal to him as if he could never bear to let him go.

"Where, Will? Where is the best place?" Sonam was deliberately talking at Will now to keep him from the sorrow he could feel welling up in his friend.

"A little further. Just a little further."

When they reached the slight bend in the river and a tiny clearing, they stopped. They did not need to agree that this was the place. Looking back, they could see the adults grouped about a hundred feet below them. Will stroked Tashi's head, whispering softly to him, his lips close to his ear. Sonam joined him and for several moments they gave Tashi their best advice, in two languages, on surviving in the wild. Then slowly Will put Tashi on the ground and pushed him away from him. The lynx ran a few yards and stopped. For a moment it looked as though he was going to run back to the boys but they shouted at him and waved their arms so that he ran into the bushes.

Sonam turned to Will. "Now I am going too." The boys smiled at each other a little awkwardly, not knowing what to say. Sonam turned and started to follow the stream up the valley.

"Sonam! Sonam! Wait!" Will ran after him. He took the amulet box from his neck and slipped it over Sonam's head. "The mantra of the Future Buddha. To protect you." And suddenly Sonam flung his arms around Will and held him tightly.

"I'll see you, Will. I'll see you again. I know I will."

Will turned away and walked slowly down the stream to rejoin the others. After a few yards, he turned to look back. Sonam was nearly at the top of the stream, walking fast. Will stared at the tiny clearing where they had released Tashi. At first it looked empty but as he stared he thought he saw the lynx, his head turning back over his shoulder before he finally disappeared amongst the trees.

Acknowledgements

Sincere thanks to Mike Krzesinski for the cover, to Debbie Young, Hannah Persaud and Andrew Stevenson for valuable input at times of need, and to Carol Armour and Neil Sutherland for early proofreading and comments.

Made in the USA
Charleston, SC
21 October 2016